"Best in Category" 2018 Chanticleer
International Book Awards

Crowned Heart of Excellence Winner –
InD'Tale Magazine

Feathered Quill Finalist

"The Warrior's Progeny" is an intense, page-turning adventure that weaves a hot contemporary romance with spell-binding Greek mythology! While the romance is the main focus of the story, a subplot occurs with characters from the first book (Dee is a hoot!) as they try to work out what is happening and what they need to do to save the gods. The main character's experience dreams in which Greek mythology is richly woven in, keeping the modern romance tethered to the past. "The Warrior's Progeny" is a thrilling ride that will have readers clamoring for the next installment!

Tricia Hill - InD'Tale Magazine

This story is about Finn and Raven, two opposites from different worlds who might just very well be connected by a root in the mythical Greek Gods. I enjoy a story that takes real world and flavors it with the supernatural/mystical. The author blends a story of romance, healing and growth, and a wee bit of the paranormal. I appreciated the characters' backstory and especially like Dee, Finn's grandmother (I love layered secondary characters). The Hawaii setting was a joy to read about and I could definitely see that this author did her research.

Jean M. Grant (Author) - Hundred Series

The Sea Archer is a remarkable undertaking. The many diverse sub-plots are a credit not only to author Heckman's talent for research but to the depths of her imagination. And when Raven finally draws the proverbial line in the sand and reclaims her life, the reader experiences a hip-swinging, foot-stomping happy dance moments—and it's worth the ride.

Kat Henry Doran - Wild Women Reviews

BOOKS BY JENY

The Heaven & Earth Series:
The Sea Archer

The Warrior's Progeny

Other Works:
"Dancing Through Tears"
(Australia Burns Anthology, Vol. 2)

Releasing the Catch

Dee's Cornucopia

Contact Information: info@celticbutterflypublishing.com
Cover Art by Steven Novak

Celtic Butterfly Publishing
PO Box 2661
Stanwood, Washington 98292-2661

Visit us at www.celticbutterflypublishing.com

Publishing History
First Edition, 2021
Print ISBN 978-0-9965096-0-2
Digital ISBN 978-0-9965096-3-3

The Heaven & Earth Series
Published in the United States of America

JENY HECKMAN

DEE'S CORNUCOPIA

A NOVELLA

CELTIC BUTTERFLY PUBLISHING

To the grandmothers who
care for their grandchildren,
as if they were their own.

Sarah, Lola, and Gloria

CHAPTER 1

"MY GOD, IT'S HOTTER than a billy goat's ass in a pepper patch out there," Dee announced as she entered the office furnished with the rich fragrance of leather, old wood, coffee, and tobacco smoke.

Her boss, Bert Norton, sat hunched at his desk, puffing on his ancient pipe. His gaze snapped to hers, and he gave the merest hint of a smile before frowning at her crass expression. The two fellows, also occupying the room, stood a little straighter at her appearance, but gave each other surreptitious glares. They wore identical uniforms of scarred leather boots, dusty work trousers and damp cotton shirts, right down to the sweat-stained field-hand hats squeezed together in their enormous fists.

"Ah, sorry?" Dee phrased it almost like a question and raised her eyebrows at the deluge of testosterone in the small space.

"Deidre, please, take a seat." Bert gestured to one of the broad wing-back chairs occupying the area in front of his desk.

The two imposing men shifted their weight from foot to foot in apparent agitation. *If I sit in that chair, I'll look weak.* Possessing a vagina created enough of a disadvantage chasm already.

"Thanks, Mr. Norton, I'll stand. No sense in giving anyone the upper hand, right?" she quipped and slapped her hands on her hips, shifting her own weight from side to side, like a metronome. The corner of her boss's lips twitched, but he sighed with heavy resignation, and they both looked over at the two workers.

One man, Beaker Sparks, of medium height, but strong, muscular build, grunted as she studied him, and frowned. The only remarkable thing about the field-hand? The size of the white-head marring his chin. His icy, steel gaze peered down a nose too long and broad for his pocked face in a way that left her feeling exposed and undressed. Though she was under-age, it didn't stop Beaker, twenty-two years her senior, from trying to step out with her since her arrival at the Sugar Grove Plantation two years prior.

However, with each rejection he became more ardent and acquisitive, until the girl reached her boiling point and punched him dead in the face when he got too handsy one day. Taken unaware by the retaliation, Beaker stumbled in front of the mixed lunch assembly and fell, appearing as if the petite creature knocked him on his ass. Afterward, the man took to impugning her character, even hinting she'd given him a gratifying blow job during a lunch break in the outhouse. Dee gave Sparks a look that suggested he wasn't worth the lump of cow shit she walked in daily, and it caused the muscles in his jaw to clench and his nostrils to flare like an Adirondack moose ready to charge.

Her eyes darted to the other man. What she discovered about him was his name… Arthur, and delicious dream boat didn't scratch the surface of his appearance. Arthur stood taller than Sparks by several inches, and Dee by more than a foot. His wide muscular shoulders and massive chest tapered down into a trim waist. Brilliant, clear blue eyes with generous dollops of gold and green encircling the pupils searched the young woman's face, captivating her attention. His mouth… that wide and generous creation by God, broke into an easy grin whenever their eyes connected across the expansive lunchroom over his short tenure at the plantation. The handsome man worked at the company a little over two weeks and labored in the fields two zones over from where she stripped sugarcane, and he worked and repaired the harvesting equipment.

The who worked with her in the fields or in its office all had eyes for the mysterious new employee, and now up close, Dee understood why. Even her best friend, Evie had the hots for him and she about to be a married woman.

"Walker," Norton barked, causing her to come out of her reverie. "These two men have been brawling over you, and it's disrupting my lunch hour."

"Really?" Dee sighed with exaggerated innocence and tilted her head to the side to consider both of them again. "Hmm." She pretended to think about it and exhaled hard through pursed lips. "Okay, well, I'm probably too young for both of 'em, but seeing as Sparks is a genuine asshole, I think I'll take the tall drink of water there." Arthur's eyes popped open wider and his eyebrows lifted.

"Ah, no, ma'am," Arthur drawled out Alabama. "I was just tellin' Mr. Norton here, that the man was speaking wicked regardin' your appearance." He jerked his chin in Sparks' direction, and venom shot out of those magnificent eyes. "There's no excuse for such language about a young lady."

The three men scanned the length of the young lady in question, and she followed their gaze. The wet heat left her bright orange work shirt clinging to her rather well-endowed bosom. Purple plaid trousers, also damp with sweat, clung to her thighs. She supposed she'd have to get used to this kind of attention now that she'd at last received her period and became a woman at the venerable age of sixteen.

"That right? Well, what's he been saying then?"

"Ah… well…" Arthur's neck and face flamed crimson, whether in anger or embarrassment, Dee couldn't decide. "Mr. Sparks here suggested that you've… ah… had relations in a public settin', and in the privy." He hesitated, and when she lifted her eyebrows to continue, he added, "Um, with several others watchin' y'all?"

Dee turned to glare at her nemesis, then at her boss. "Well, I can't fault his imagination, now can I? I wonder what Mama would have to say about that, Mr. Norton?" She turned back to her boss, eyebrows lifted. "An older gentleman makin' advances at her naïve underage daughter?" Dee cocked her head to the side again, as if thinking, then answered her own question. "Oh yeah, she'd say, 'Dee, sweetheart, next time that weasel Sparks opens his mouth, don't bother punching him in the face, kick him the balls instead. That'll make his lips pucker to the size of a ladybug's butt'."

"No, your mama would wash out your filthy mouth with soap and tell you to stop leading guys on," Sparks spat in his high-pitched nasal register, then turned toward their boss, as Arthur's fists clenched in reflex. "You gonna believe this, sir? I ain't never…"

"Naw," Dee retorted, interrupting what she knew would be a load of horse shit, and stepped forward to stare down the jackass, with all the supremacy her small stature could muster. "It's 1958, Beak. Mama would say break a foot off in the fool's fucking ass."

With that, she drew back her booted foot and kicked him with exactitude in the center of his scrotum. All three men groaned in immediate solidarity, and Arthur's powerful arm snaked around her tiny waist, lifting her body from the floor in restraint. She kicked out again, clipping her nemesis's chin, and popped his pimple. Beaker Sparks wheezed, clutching the most offended area, and gave an uncontrolled fart as he writhed around on the industrial carpet. Arthur set Dee back on her feet and stood between her and the fallen man, as she returned her attention to Norton.

"Okay, so I guess we're done here then… right?" Without waiting for his stunned response, she spun around and punched out the door, calling, "That's real good too 'cause it's time to get back to work."

The whistle announced the lunch hour conclusion, two seconds after she raised a finger to point at it.

Deidre Georgette Walker lived an adventurous life in her sixteen years. Her mother, Catherine, explained the story of her terrifying entrance into the world on December 7, 1941, on the island of Oahu, many times over the course of her brief life. As echoes of the aerial torpedoes hitting the Pacific Fleet ten miles away ricocheted off the walls, only a single neighbor lady attended the childbirth. Catherine always maintained, with tears in her eyes, Dee entered the world, just as her father, George, a Chief Watertender aboard the *USS Arizona*, left it in a watery tomb.

Now, Dee stretched her back and glanced over the distant fields, unseeing. The photograph on her mother's bed stand with an image of her father in full dress uniform filled her mind instead. The enigmatic ghost who one day would have… should have… taught her how to fight off men like Beaker Sparks. However, fate never allowed her that paternal protection. Staring down at weather roughened hands, she sighed. The malodorous scent from the pre-harvest fires filled her nostrils, and she wrinkled her nose. Wanting to rid herself of the stink, she tilted her head up to the sunshine and radiant bright blue sky. A thin line of black smoke coiled and unfurled, blemishing the pristine canvas, and she frowned. Her thoughts wandered back to the previous interlude.

Dee imagined Norton calling up her mother, now owner and operator of the successful, Akua Wahine Floral and Gifts, in Koloa, about what transpired in his office. *Oh, how I'd like to be a butterfly on the wall for that conversation.* She giggled.

Catherine came to the island of Kauai distraught and overwhelmed after the attack on Pearl Harbor. She inquired into a job at the plantation when Dee was just six months old. Bert Norton took one look at the beautiful broken woman and love at first sight blossomed, or so her mother told her. When they fell on hard times and Dee inquired about her own job, Mama demanded two things from her boss if her offspring worked for him. The first, immediate notification should something like what just happened, happen. The other being equal wages to that of any male peer in her same position and experience. If Catherine Walker's daughter made the grown-up decision to go to work, by God, Bertrum D. Norton would ante up for the sacrifice.

Dee grinned at her stalwart boss's blush and puppy eyes whenever he gazed upon her mama. *Yep, the eldest Miss Walker had that man wrapped around her little ole pinkie toe.*

"I meant no offense," Arthur asserted, causing Dee to jump out of her musings. She turned to look at him with a hand to her chest.

"Damn, Arthur, you scared me."

"Sorry."

The afternoon whistle blew again, and groans rose into a cacophony of misery across the acreage. She started for the light rail and small train that transported the workers to and from the various zones in the fields. Pulling her damp shirt away from her ribcage, it made an odd sucking noise, and she could smell her own sweat.

Dee glanced over at the man, but he just held his field hat in his hands and paced her stride. He considered the fields rather than her face, before mumbling, "I just thought he shouldn't be speakin' that way about you is all."

The train pulled in, and the workers jumped onto the flatbeds. The couple jogged to catch up to it and jumped on together as it lurched forward.

When they settled into comfortable positions, he gave her a side eye. "Why's a little gal like you working full time here rather than at school with kids your own age?"

She considered the question, then gave him a brief summary of the circumstances that led her there. "Mama said it was crazy on Oahu right after the attacks. Martial law was in effect and everyone and everything was just devastated. We got stranded on Waikiki for weeks after, and terrified more attacks would come, Mama moved us here. She ain't never left since."

"Golly, that's a pretty brave woman there, if ya ask me. I think I'd like to meet your mama someday."

"She sure is," Dee agreed with pride. "Had her grief, then had me on top of it, but I'll be damned if she didn't pull up her bootstraps and get to work. She found a secretarial job with Mr. Norton himself, but even then, she had to work real hard to make ends meet. The Navy didn't confirm Daddy's death for real until I was seven years old."

"Was she born here?"

"Here? Naw. Mama only ever was a farmer from Charter Oak, Iowa. They came to Hawaii, after Daddy got stationed here."

Dee watched the fields spread out before her. "We got in bad straights, financially. So, a couple of years ago, I decided I could help Mama out. Norton would do anything for her and said I could work for him. After a year of nose to the grindstone, we were back on our feet. Mama told me I had to go back to school, but I loved what I was doing, and as they say, the same boiling water that softens a potato can harden an egg."

He gave her an incredulous look. "What in the hell're you talkin' about?"

"Oh." She blushed. "I'm just explainin' how I'm as stubborn as a cow deciding to take a shit. It's just gonna happen and Mama knows it." Arthur guffawed, and she chuckled despite herself. "She didn't like it at all, but she knew I made my mind up. I wanted her to have her dream. So, she took out a small loan with Mr. Norton and opened the prettiest floral shop you ever saw, while I stayed on here. We've been doing pretty good ever since."

"By God, you're sassy. My mama would've hided my ass for back talkin'."

"Mine's been known to do that, too, but she knew my mind and knew I'd had enough of school. She hates that I'm exposed to the likes of Sparks, but she also knows I can handle myself just fine."

Dee's face faltered a bit, because life wasn't exactly turning out how she envisioned it, nor did it appear to venture back on track for some time to come. She cast a glance at the young man, as he turned those magnetic eyes toward hers.

"You want to take me out to the picture show tonight, Arthur?"

"I... what?"

"There's this Eva Gabor flick I want to see. Something with initials... I don't remember the name of it right off."

"GiGi?"

Dee snapped her fingers twice and pointed at him, "Yep that's the one."

"Shouldn't I be the one to ask you out?" Arthur suggested, giving her another sideways glance.

"Nah," Dee shrugged. "I figure why waste time. You're a handsome man... seems like you'd be respectful enough and not try anything fresh."

"With you?" He laughed. "I wouldn't dream of it. You scare the absolute hell out of me."

She grinned at him as he made a study of her face. "All right, well, I'm at 510 Hoona Road, just a little way down from Po'ipū beach. How about 7:30?"

"All right, it's a date."

"Good." When her stop came, she jumped off the platform, calling, "And Arthur?" She turned to face him, walking backward as the train ground its machinery forward once more. He didn't answer, just continued to stare at her. "Take a bath first, 'cause you smell like sweat and bad decisions."

A slow smile transformed his face, and he tipped his hat, "Yes, ma'am."

Chuckling, she gave a wave, and the train pushed forward.

"Mama?" Dee called out when she arrived home and let the screen door snap back with a bang. She sprinted into the kitchen where her mother stood at the stove tasting some red sauce from a wooden spoon. Content with the taste, the older woman placed the spoon back in the sauce and lowered the heat a little.

"Deidre Georgette, I've told you time and time again not to let that screen door bang closed like that."

"Sorry, Mama, but guess what?"

"What?" She withdrew Dee's patchwork hat off her head, watching the wheat-colored locks fall across her shoulders in messy waves, before securing it on the hook by the backdoor. Catherine turned and examined her daughter's flushed face.

"Arthur asked me out to the movies tonight."

"Arthur?" Catherine frowned, "Arthur, who?"

"Hmm." Dee tilted her head to the side thinking. "You know, I don't reckon I've ever been told his surname." She drew her brows together. "Huh. I don't know, but it's that new boy I was telling you about at work, with the dreamy eyes and cute butt."

"Deidre, you are not going to the movies with some man you don't even know the name of."

"Oh, I know his name, Mama, just not his last name." She turned to the sink and washed her hands. "You'll never guess what he did for me, though."

"I want to hear, but first, tell me what happened today. Mr. Norton…"

"It's all part of the same thing." As her daughter relayed the events that transpired, Catherine's brow creased deeper. "So, I said, on second thought you'd tell me to break a foot off in his fucking ass…"

"Deidre!"

"Sorry, Mama, but ya gotta talk like that, or those types of men won't even listen. They'll just do as they please." Catherine's brow furrowed again as she shook her head in helpless disapproval, and Dee kissed her soft cheek. "It's okay, Mama. Ole' Beaker Sparks didn't know what hit him and Arthur, he's a genuine gentleman."

"Well, what time is the gentleman caller coming?"

"About 7:30." Dee glanced up at the clock. "Damn, that's about an hour. I gotta take a bath." She moved toward the hallway, walking backward, and called out, "You'll like this, too, Mama. I told ole Arthur he had to take a bath too before he came over here, 'cause he smelled like sweat and bad decisions. You should've seen his face, could have knocked him over with a feather."

Catherine tried to conceal a smile as her little spitfire skipped down the hall. With a chuckle, she gave a shake of her head, and rolled her eyes to Heaven. *Forget Dee, God help Arthur, whoever.*

CHAPTER 2

Arthur Taylor walked into the mess hall on his third day of employment, with his friend, Maleko Ho and a new co-worker, Issac Lindell, when his eyes fell upon the most beautiful gal he'd ever seen. She sat on top of a picnic table and kept court with a few ladies he recognized as fellow field workers.

Her long, thick ponytail, the color of golden-wheat, held secure under a sunshine-yellow kerchief, swayed back and forth on her back like a metronome. Large, luminous bluebell eyes came into his field of vision when she turned to assess everything around her while she spoke and gestured in animation with her hands. Her work overalls displayed a vivid patchwork of colors that bordered on ridiculous, as the bib hugged a magnificent bosom.

Every now and again she checked men who cat-called or expressed a lewd act toward the women by extending her middle finger or offering her own coarse retort. He fell in love with her on the spot.

"Who's that little gal over there?" Arthur asked the men without taking his eyes from her.

Maleko craned his neck to see where the tall man nodded and grinned. "Well, that's Dee Walker. I've known her since what… elementary school? I haven't seen her for years. *Damn,* she turned into a dish."

"Jailbait, more like," Issac observed. "Don't touch her, she's only sixteen, and her mother would set the police on you so fast, you wouldn't know what hit you. And Norton… he's her guard dog. He'd fire your ass in a hot minute."

"Who's her mama?" Arthur asked.

"Catherine Walker," Issac replied. "She used to be Norton's secretary and ran everything around here with an iron fist. She opened a flower shop somewhere in town about a year ago. Dee's been here a couple of years now. Beaker Spark's the only one who's tried anything and the only reason he ain't got fired yet is I expect Mr. Norton hasn't heard about it yet." Issac eyed the taller of his new co-workers. "She and Evie are pretty good friends."

"Evie?" Maleko asked.

"My girl." He pointed to a taller woman with a ponytail of chestnut hair standing next to Dee.

Arthur continued to stare as his friends chuckled and left him standing there alone. Seeming to sense his gaze, Dee's eyes connected with his and held. She gave him a radiant smile, and he grinned back as the bell signaled the return to work. The break room exploded into movement, and she disappeared into the crowd.

Over the next couple of weeks, he observed Dee from afar. Her unique personality entertained even the surliest of men, which captivated the young Alabama man even more. She was a burst of color in the monochromatic tones all around her.

However, he wasn't alone in his attraction. Beaker Sparks stood out among the throng of admirers. His observations regarding her were often graphic and crude as he tried to dim her hue. So, being the well brought up man his mother raised, Arthur couldn't help but defend her honor, especially after he learned her age. His anger roiled at its threshold, then spewed over when Beaker, a man old enough to be the girl's father, implied he'd taken Dee on the hood of his car. Lunging at the man, he socked him in the mouth and continued to pound on him until several men nearby pulled them apart.

By the time the trio collided in Norton's office, Arthur discovered the sixteen-year-old pixie could more than take care of herself when she booted her bully in the balls.

My God, but she was glorious in her rage. He stood at his mirror in tan cotton slacks and an undershirt tank, grinning at the memory, as he created a perfect ducktail in his dishwater blonde locks. Picking up his pressed white button-up, he threaded long, muscular arms through the sleeves, before tucking in the shirt and doing up its buttons. He slipped on polished loafers, before snatching up his wallet and car keys, all the while whistling, *All I Have to Do is Dream*, anticipating a great spring evening.

Dee peered at her reflection in the chipped, oval mirror suspended above her bathroom sink by a coarse, golden ribbon. Thank God she didn't have to work too hard to appear decent. A little mascara, some red lipstick, ten minutes under her Lilly Dache's bonnet blow dryer with some well-placed curlers and voila. Her youthful exuberance, better than any cream or potion, elevated her reflection and self-esteem.

She reached for her bottle of Grape Nehi and took a sip. As the tangy bite of soda slid over her tongue and down her throat, a peculiar emotion blew over her. She drew a quick intake of breath and lifted her head to the mirror again.

The reflection, though still her face, seemed to have an overlay of another's but she couldn't quite capture the specific attributes in her mind. Her stomach swirled with butterflies and energy sizzled up her spine as the tiny room spun. A fullness flowed into her frontal lobe, causing it to expand and sharpen, as the large banyan tree outside her home called to her. The same sensations occurred many times since she counted five years of age. Traversing from her room to the back yard, she stood under the tree, but stared out over the ocean.

The salty waves moved in rhythm with her blood and inside, her body rose, crested and fell with the water. Arthur's smiling face suffused through the cells of her body. Their hands joined, their lips met, and a sense of union flushed through her on a second wave before settling once more. Breathless, Dee blinked, and the waves returned to crash against the shore. She took in the length of the wise banyan tree and grinned, before spinning in a circle and skipping back into the house.

"You clean up well," Dee opened the screen door to her date twenty minutes later.

His blond hair glistened under the porch lights, and his eyes drank in the bodice of her dress, clinging to her curves and waist before releasing into a full skirt. Bright pink and periwinkle plumeria flowers covered its surface and complemented her creamy tan.

"Dee," he said, ruffled. "Ya look like an enormous flower." He blushed and appeared to want to crawl under the welcome mat. "I mean, I reckon you're as pretty as a dove."

"Thank you."

"Deidre?" her mother called, wiping her hands on her apron, as she walked out from the kitchen and approached the couple. "Oh, hello." She extended her hand and scrutinized the caller. "I'm Catherine Walker, Dee's mama."

"Ma'am," Arthur said and shook her hand. "I'm Arthur Taylor."

"Mm hmm," she replied. "And how old are *you*, Arthur Taylor?"

"Mama," Dee warned, but Arthur just smiled at the dragon at the gate.

"No, that's fine. I turned eighteen just this past May ma'am, and I promise you I won't break your trust with the honor of your daughter."

"Oh, like hell," Dee snorted, and drew her brows together, then grabbed his hand and tried to pull him back through the open door.

"It's not *you* I'm worried about, Mr. Taylor," Catherine retorted, as the couple traversed the threshold. She turned a castigating glare on her daughter. "Behave yourself, Deidre Georgette," she hissed, then glanced up at the man. "Not too late now, Arthur."

"No, ma'am," the suitor confirmed. Dee turned back and kissed the apple of her mother's soft cheek.

"Well, okay. Let's go." Dee giggled, as she slid across the bench seat of his dusty pick-up, to sit next to him. "So, how did you get to Hawai'i from wherever you're from?"

"Alabama." Arthur smiled down at her and turned the key in the ignition. The truck clucked to life. "First off, where to?"

"Oh, um." Dee closed her eyes and tilted her head back, thinking. "You know where Maggie's drive-in is?"

"Sure do. Burgers it is." The couple started driving the thirty minutes into Waimea, "So, to answer your question, I'm from Tuscaloosa, Alabama. I graduated in '57 and started workin' at my daddy's factory along with my six brothers."

"Six!"

"Yeah, I'm the baby." He ran a hand through his hair. "Well, I hated every minute in there, just starin' at metal and brick all damn day. Oh," he said, as if realizing he'd cursed. "Sorry."

"You've gotta get over that, if we're gonna hang out, Arthur. I'm not gonna censor my shit, damns, and fucks. So, you aren't offending me."

"All right then." He tried not to laugh before resuming his story. "So, Daddy expected me to work there with him, and when I didn't, he told me to light out."

"So, you just up and left your entire family?"

"Pa expected me to follow in his footsteps. It's what we do, and I tried, that's the God's honest truth. But I just couldn't," he explained. "I wanted more than just a livin' behind the four walls of a factory, day in and day out." He glanced down at her as he shifted gears, eyes in hopeful understanding. "See, it made him old and ornery, before his time, ya know? I wanted outdoors and sunshine. Just, freedom... So, I left."

"What did your dad do?"

"He cut all ties with me. Said if I was gonna waste my life, and abandon my family, I didn't have any kin in Alabama no more." He shrugged. "Don't matter… the only person I really miss is Mama."

"And she just let all that happen?"

"Wasn't much she could do. Things are different over there."

Excited for his new life, Dee bounced in her seat a little. "What happened then?"

"Well, I worked my way to California, living in my car. I got a job with Matson, the freight company?" She nodded her understanding of the company. "This last July, they were lookin' for able-bodied men to make the long haul and unload supplies on a freighter here." He grinned, thinking about the sense of adventure he'd had. "I signed up right away and worked on the *S.S. Hawai'ian Light.*"

"San Francisco to Hilo?"

"Now, how did you know that?"

"I'm not stupid."

"Oh," he chuckled, "Okay, I'll remember that."

"What happened next?"

"Well, we pulled in and I saw that big, misty harbor, with the mountains pokin' out the top. All that white sand, palm trees and the deep blue color of my first Hawai'ian sky. It was the first day of spring and pretty as a picture. Well, it dazzled me." He glanced over at her and smiled. "Kind of like you." She grinned back. "I collected my paycheck then and there and abandoned ship."

"How did you get your job at Sugar Grove?"

"I've always been able to understand most any machine put in front of me. Those new sugarcane harvesters are somethin' to see, I tell you what. I knew I chose right with bein' outdoors and loved workin' out in the fields. I met Maleko Ho and…"

"Maleko Ho?"

"Yeah."

"Huh. I remember him from the third grade. He was a couple years ahead of me in school."

"Yeah, he told me that. Well, anyway, he was there for the weekend and we started pal'in' around. In the end, he talked me into comin' over here to Kaua'i."

"Yeah, their family has lived here a long time."

He nodded in acknowledgment. "It only took me a few days to realize I liked it even better here. His daddy knew Mr. Norton and got us both work at the plantation." The lights of the drive-in glowed in the windshield. "And here we are."

They settled into a booth inside and talked more about work and the area they called home, while dining on thick, juicy cheeseburgers and hot crispy fries. Content, Arthur wiped his mouth, leaned back in the seat, and sipped his Coca-Cola, while eyeing his date over the bottle.

"So, what about you, little dove?"

"What about me?"

"How *does* a little sixteen-year-old gal like you wind up workin' for a sugar plantation, rather than be in school kissin' boys?"

"I already told ya." Dee grinned. "And who says I ain't been kissing no boys?"

"Well," Arthur barked out a laugh, "I sure couldn't fault them."

Dee giggled and sipped her water. "Ya know, when the war spread on over to Korea, this place was crawling with all the new servicemen. The island was just busting at the seams and they needed more field workers and farmers just to feed them all. Oahu and the Big Island already had its share of tourists, but quite a few popped up over here too. Price of living skyrocketed, and that's why Mama couldn't keep the house off Po'ipū anymore. Not on her salary alone, anyway. Well, I just couldn't let that happen."

"So being the headstrong gal you are, you quit school and helped your mama with the expenses?" He gave a shake of his head at the sacrifice. "Then you come to work and have the likes of Beaker Sparks pawin' at ya."

"Oh, please, the day I can't handle Beaker is a sad, sad day." She gave an airy wave of her hand. "He's nothing."

"But you must want something more than this someday. What's your dream?"

Her entire face transformed and glowed as she smiled, eyes brightening. "I want to have my own shop."

"Shop?"

"Yeah, I want to have a huge nursery, with all kinds of vegetables and flowers. Maybe have a little gift shop attached. Then I'm going to get the brightest and most crazy muumuus there are and wear 'em every day, with flowers all up in my hair." She waved her hands around her head, indicating some outlandish style.

"I can see ya just like that. The sun all up in your hair and gold all around ya. Christ almighty, that makes a picture."

She blushed at the compliment, but said almost dream-like, "Someday… that's what I want to do. Be my own boss and have my own business. It's gonna happen… you just wait and see."

That night, Arthur found a depth to Dee that maligned her years and education and not only found attraction but genuine friendship. When they drove back home through the inky night, Dee slid across the bench seat once more to sit beside him. She took his arm and placed it around her shoulders as she shifted the gears of his truck for him.

"Did you have fun?" Arthur asked as they drove on the open highway.

"I did… a lot. Thanks for taking me."

"Well, you didn't give me much choice now, did ya?" he said, gazing down his nose at her.

"Aw, hell," Dee chortled. "It would've taken you forever to ask me out, and you know it. I just made it easier on you."

"That ya did, sassy dove," he chuckled.

"You know what, Arthur?" Dee said, as he pulled into the Walker driveway and turned off the lights and engine.

He shifted in his seat to look at her. "What's that?"

"You and me, we're gonna get married someday. The water was behaving funny when I got home earlier, and I seen it coming."

"Ah." He drew his brows together in consternation and peered out at the garage before looking back to her, at a loss for what to address first.

She snorted and laid a hand on his cheek, turning it to face her again. "I'm like a sensitive… a seer. Do you know what that is?"

"I… ah… no," he admitted, and scanned her eyes, hopeful for a punchline.

"Sometimes, things come to me in weird ways. It's been happening to me since I was about five years old. It started off just kind of knowing things sometimes."

"Like?"

"Like, telling Mama to go around the block because a parking space would open up for her in perfect time. Or sometimes I get some images and a feeling. Like, I didn't know it would be you until tonight when I got home from work, but you *are* the one." Complete bafflement must have shown on his face, and he searched for something to say. Dee smiled in reassurance. "I don't want you to worry though."

"Oh," he said, surprised because he'd been trying to work out that very thing. "I-I can't say I'm worried as much as… just… um…"

"Yeah, well, it's not gonna happen for another couple of years yet."

"Couple of years?" he echoed. "Why's that?"

"Because I'm only sixteen, silly, and I'm gonna wait until I'm eighteen to have some of the intercourse." She spoke the last word in syllables.

Arthur's mouth dropped open as she tried what she must have thought looked like a seductive smile. It came across looking like an adorable duck, and one corner of his mouth twitched up. Dee surprised him more when she climbed onto his lap and straddled his hips. Placing hands on either side of his aghast face, on a level with her lovely breasts, she tilted his face up to hers. Her scent filled the cabin of his truck. He breathed in shallow gasps as she lowered her mouth to his and kissed him with unexpected passion. Arthur experienced the most delicious tug in his belly and his penis jerked, then hardened in his pants underneath her. Realization blossomed on her face, and she grinned, kissing him once more.

"Sorry," she gasped as they broke apart. "I just had to do that. It'll be hard on both of us, I expect, but I promise once I have two years to work my way up to the notion, I think I'll be damn good at it."

Panting, Arthur pushed her hair back from her face and tucked it behind her ears. "Yeah," he confirmed in a strangled voice, "I expect so, darlin'. Now, let me take ya to the door, before all the neighbors see us, and your reputation, and my good word to your mama, get ruined forever."

CHAPTER 3

DECEMBER 1962

THE WINTER DEE TURNED twenty-one, Arthur drove his wife and her mother to a large lot a scant distance inland from Po'ipū beach. In the northwest corner of the acreage, a large "For Sale" sign stood erect, next to a sixteen-hundred square-foot home. As the trio got out of the car, Dee observed her surroundings, then Arthur in confusion.

"What's all this then?"

"Old man Kahale's gonna go live in with his son on the Northside. They're sellin' all of this." Catherine's mouth dipped into an immediate frown and glanced at the house.

Dee eyed her mother, then scanned the area. "But we have the house on the water, with Mama. You wanna move already?"

Upon their wedding, two years earlier, Catherine suggested Arthur move in with them, rather than finding property or buying another house. The couple loved the idea and merely added a larger bedroom and en suite to the Walker house.

"Oh, no." Arthur hurried over to the two women in reassurance, grabbing each by a hand. "I think we're all enjoyin' the arrangement, aren't we?" He searched the older woman's face. "Unless you're ready for us to leave, Mama?"

A relieved smile slid onto Catherine's face as she shook her head, and he wrapped arms around her shoulders, while turning both their bodies toward his bride. "No, see, I talked with the son, I think his name's Pika, and he just wants rid of it." He kissed the top of his mother-in-law's head and took a few steps away from her, gesturing wide with his arms. "They built the house in 1913, and it needs some work, but overall, Kahale took great care of the place."

"Why is Kahale selling?" Catherine inquired.

"He just said it's too much land for him to maintain anymore. I went 'round to the bank yesterday, and we qualify for a decent loan." Still confused, Dee looked around, so he clarified, "Honey, you can have your little farmer's market." He gazed out over the rolling land, hunched down to her height and pointed. "Look here, you can put in some gardens over there and grow the flowers Mama needs for the floral shop. Hell, she can move her shop out here too, so she doesn't have to pay that high rent in Koloa anymore. You'll have the land to do whatever you want. On the weekends and evenings, Maleko and I can get some equipment up in here and do any work that needs doin'."

"You could turn the house there into a gift shop and office," Catherine suggested, warming to the idea. "Just like you wanted, Dee. And I have some money saved and…"

"No, Mama," Arthur said with gentle authority. "I don't want you to have to do anything. You've done enough for us already."

"But you'll be saving *me* money on the shop, and by growing the flowers here, we could make our own varieties."

"Well, I'll leave that up to you and Dee to decide," Arthur said, turning to his wife and grinning. "Happy Birthday, little dove."

"Oh, Arthur, this is incredible," Catherine proclaimed, and to her daughter said, "Well? What do you think, sweetheart?"

Dumbfounded, Dee gaped at her husband in awe. "You did all this for me?" The warm glow suffused her cells, and she felt the heat of it flush her face.

"Well, yes, but I'd say we're all gonna benefit from it. I don't like you workin' out there in the fields, darlin'. All that blisterin' sun. You'd be happier here, wouldn't ya?" Dee launched herself in his arms, and delighted he swung her around, laughing. When he set her on her feet again, he asked, "Okay, well now that's settled. What are you going to name her?"

She took in the broad expanse of the property and breathed in a deep joyful lungful of air before replying on the exhale, "Dee's Cornucopia."

Dee spent the next couple of years transforming the property into an Eden and the dwelling into her office and gift shop. Much like the owner, Dee's Cornucopia contained a happy, vibrant quality about it, full of fragrant colors and fun activities. Arthur built a small playground and an outbuilding for Catherine's floral shop, the Calico Cupboard. It included an enclosed greenhouse and storage room, but also added a tea-room for extra revenue, and the two women combined all their assets to create one promising business. Dee even hired her best friend, Evie, out of the fields and set her to work as the gift shop manager.

The September evening sparkled as Dee shoveled dirt into a new raised flower bed, installed for the specific purpose of cultivating a special cross-variety of roses. Joy thrummed low in her chest, as a tiny butterfly landed on the border trim around the bed. She paused, but the butterfly didn't appear to be in a hurry to fly away.

A wave of vertigo flushed throughout her system. Reaching out a hand to steady herself, thousands of butterflies erupted from the soil, and Dee jolted at the invasion. The beautiful insects fluttered around her so thick, she couldn't see through them and laughed. As they trailed away, she staggered to her feet and ran after them to the large cornucopia display in the center of her gardens. Breathless, she eyed the tiny, magical creatures in wonder as they floated on the breeze, and their small wings fluttered against her skin. A fluid movement caused her gaze to shift downward, where a long thin snake with iridescent scales circled and coiled into a complicated knot, only to slither out of it again. The reptile repeated the action several times before disappearing into the dirt.

Dee blinked, and the butterflies winged away, their strong flutter now contained within her womb. Looking around, she noticed nothing in her surroundings stirred, and Evie, who coiled a hose nearby, didn't flinch in wonder or notice the insect invasion. She slid hands up her belly and spun around in delirious glee.

Arthur arrived at the Cornucopia an hour later and found his wife staring out over the bountiful space she created. Something about her seemed different. Supreme contentment radiated over her lovely face. He grinned at her happiness. Her declaration years earlier came true, and she indeed only wore colorful muumuus now, something the tourists loved, and the community embraced as her trademark. Today, hot pink, cobalt blue and lime green, with orange, yellow and purple flowers, splashed out from her garment, and her thick beautiful hair waved boundless and free down her back. The look fit his young bride's personality to perfection. However, she'd stayed out in the sun too long again and burned the bridge of her nose and forehead.

"I've got to buy you a hat," he whispered into her ear, as he wrapped brawny arms around her waist. She leaned back onto his broad chest. "Hello, my sassy dove. You look mighty peaceful. Pleasant day?"

"The best day," she murmured back, "After all, it's not every day you find out you're pregnant." Arthur drew his brows together, then froze. His protective arms tightened around her, but she turned to face him.

"What?" he asked, breath punching out from his lungs. "Are ya sure, darlin'?"

"Yep," Dee said, and a wide grin split across her face. "The butterflies told me."

"That's… I'm sorry, what?" Arthur began, then closed his mouth, at a loss.

It wasn't the first-time Dee spoke something outlandish to him. In fact, she experienced several "episodes" that had come to fruition since that first night he'd taken her to the movies, and she called herself a sensitive.

However, they didn't work all the time, and many times she just received a vague awareness of something on the horizon. A pragmatic man by nature, Arthur never could wrap his head around the visions, but because he loved her, he tried very hard to support her… uniqueness. This time, however, he wanted concrete fact, rather than something sensitive based.

"The butterflies, darlin'?"

"Yeah." She grabbed his hand, pulling him further into the garden, and to the massive cornucopia displayed in its center. "I was standing right here this morning, and thousands of these beautiful butterflies flew all around me, and then this snake came and made a weird circle thing."

"A snake?" he asked with skepticism, then offered, "Honey, there aren't any snakes in the Hawai'ian Islands."

"Hmm," Dee drew her brows together in thought. "Yeah, you're right. That's weird, isn't it?"

"That's the weirdest thing here?" he grinned.

"No," she giggled. "I own that I'm a weirdo, but I'm a pregnant weirdo, I'll bet my sweet ass on it." She gazed into his brilliant eyes and discovered the starburst inside them sparkled with excitement. "Don't worry, I've got an appointment set up for tomorrow morning to make sure, but wrap your head around the notion you knocked me up." He kissed the tip of her nose and wished for it to be true.

The next day dawned, and Arthur woke late, missed the turn to the plantation, and kept going to the wrong field. So, for the first time in his life, he left work early, and drove to the Cornucopia, parking his truck outside Catherine's shop. The bell over the door chimed as he strode into the fragrant, air-conditioned room.

"Mama," he called out to the void, and the elderly woman came around the corner, threading creamy white orchids onto a string. A broad grin stretched across her face as she recognized her son-in-law, and stretched up, allowing him to kiss her cheek.

"Have you heard anything yet? It's been an absolute madhouse in here today."

"No, not yet. I figured I'd buy her some celebration flowers and, if it isn't our time yet, well, then they might ease her disappointment a little."

"A fine idea," she sang. "Here now, have a look around as I finish up this lei. Just be a sec."

"No rush," he replied, glancing around. "Take your time."

He walked amidst the aromatic and vibrant displays. The woman created masterpiece after masterpiece, just like her daughter. The forced air caused a movement in his periphery, causing his attention to shift. High on the wall floated the biggest, floppiest gardening hat he'd ever seen. A colorful purple organza band encircled its brim, as a large colorful butterfly, attached on a wire, bobbed up and down with the fan. The millinery screamed Dee, and Arthur laughed out loud, breaking the silence. Catherine shuffled back to him a few minutes later, and he gestured to the headwear.

"Oh, honey, that's not for sale, it's just some old hat I found at the beach. I thought I'd make it into a prop."

"It'd be perfect for her though, don't ya think?" His mother-in-law contemplated the object, as he continued, "Yesterday she burned her nose again, and I thought I should get her something to protect her face."

The woman's eyes softened at him and declared, "Well, it sure suits her personality, doesn't it?" Arthur grinned and nodded. "That girl has no sense when she's out in her garden, gets it from me, I guess. Go on then." She nodded, and he removed the hat and the crazy butterfly from the wall, snickering. "Okay, here now, let me see that. I think we can do it one better."

Dee floated back to her nursery. She and Arthur would have a baby in early summer. She thrust the car into park, seized her paisley patchwork tote bag, and ran inside her mother's shop.

"Mama," she called out. "You're never gonna guess what."

"You were right?"

Dee spun around, and her tall, handsome husband stood holding the most beautiful and extravagant sunhat she'd ever seen. The eight-inch braided brim, in multi colors of brown, seemed to possess every flower the island contained. A ridiculous butterfly boinked out over the front on a long wire. He walked over to her and placed it on her head, and as the weight of it sank down on her cranium, the brim shaded a face, glowing with excitement.

"You are a weirdo, honey," Arthur stated, and Dee's mother chuckled behind him. "But, you're my beautiful, crazy weirdo. Never stop being that." He gripped her chin and tilted her head up, "I love you... Mama." He kissed the tip of her nose.

Dee's eyes stung a little, as she wrapped her arms around his neck and drew him in. "I love you too... Daddy," she replied. "I'm not sure if I've ever said thank you for getting me."

"It's not that hard to understand ya," he said, placing a large, roughened hand over her flat belly. "That's gonna be one lucky kid, I'm tellin' ya right now."

June 12, 1966, Dee gave birth to George Matthew Taylor. The couple called him Matty and planted another banyan tree in the opposite corner of the backyard to mark the occasion, as the final cog of their idyllic life clicked into place.

CHAPTER 4

OCTOBER 1967

ON THE LAST DAY of the harvest, Arthur woke early, eager for the busy day. He dressed in the quiet of their darkened room, before walking toward the bedroom door. Dee's hat laid with pride on the chair next to her side of the bed, and he smiled at it. He'd replaced the old one on Mother's Day, after the first one wore out, and his wife took to putting newer and crazier things in it every day since he gave it to her. Arthur's eyes found the bed and its occupants.

Fussy all night from cutting an angry and tenacious tooth, Matthew fell asleep around three AM. Exhausted from several sleepless nights, Dee surrendered and brought him into their room. Now, the baby played with the Sandman deep in his dreams and nestled into the curve of his mother's body. Arthur's eyes shifted to Dee's ethereal face. Long lashes floated across her skin in sleep, and her blonde hair laid tousled in all directions around her creamy complexion. Smitten, the man walked over to her and leaned down to plant a gentle kiss on her brow.

"Mmm." She stirred and opened her blue eyes to his. "You off then, honey? You need me to make you a little breakfast before you go?"

"No, you need to get more sleep. You're tuckered out, dove." Dee smiled at him and nodded. He knelt and whispered, "Hey, how 'bout we get Mama to watch Matty tonight? We can go see a picture show. I hear there's a corker out."

"Then come back for a tumble in the sheets?"

"Sounds like my kind of date."

Dee gave a soft chuckle before adding with a smile, "Love you."

"Love you too, my sassy dove," he murmured into her hair, and kissed her again. "See y'all tonight then." Arthur stood and left his family to their dreams.

The long, shanks of the cutting arms of the harvester jutted out like a snowplow. The mechanisms that twirled the shanks to cut and pull up the sugarcane stalks jammed. Sluggish all morning, the system settled into failure. Bert Norton, who must've woken up on the wrong side of the bed himself, sliced through his employees with a sharp tongue about the costly time delays.

Arthur jumped down from the driving compartment to once more repair the mechanism and landed on a large rock, causing his knee to pop one direction and his foot to pop in the other. The offended areas exploded with pain.

"Ah, shit," he grunted and attempted to stand, swinging his arm up to catch hold of the stationary vehicle for support. The distracted co-worker in the cab, unable to see over the wheel house, took the wave for assent to continue driving, and shoved the stick shift into gear. The vehicle lurched forward in an angry stutter.

As the forty-thousand-pound machine rolled toward him, Arthur yelled for the man to stop, slapping a hand on the metal, before trying to hop out of the way. When he set his leg down and placed his full weight on the wounded appendage, it buckled in pain and he fell to the earth. Arthur's mind jerked into a series of life flashes, with just a moment to appreciate the life he lived and was about to lose. As the machine ground him into the flattened soil, the pressure to his mid-section released oxygen from his body. Numbness spread out from his center and moved along his limbs, as his spine gave a series of pops, sinking deeper into the sugar cane stalks.

Maleko must have seen the horror unfold, for he slapped a hand on the door of the harvester and screamed at the driver to stop. His friend's concerned face flooded Arthur's vision, as if behind a darkening gauzy veil.

"Arthur!" he screamed. "Arthur, can you hear me? We're getting you help, man, just hang on, hang on."

Arthur searched his friend's face, but everything moved in slow motion. Maleko's face, so close to his own, grew even darker, and it sounded like someone turned down the volume on the world. Only his erratic heartbeat thumped in his brain in loud rapport. Off in the distance, someone screamed. Faces loomed over him, all reflecting what he already knew. His eyes lolled to one side, where the driver of the harvester hovered on hands and knees, regurgitating the contents of his stomach in the nearby stalks. The fool had killed him.

"Dee," Arthur croaked as thick blood gurgled into his lungs and out of his mouth. "S-Stop…" He tried to gasp, but pin-pricked explosions within caused him to convulse with each new detonation. His brilliant eyes turned upward and took in the last thing they'd ever see, the summer blue of the Hawai'ian sky.

Dee jerked the gray shirt down so it snapped in the wind, before securing it to the line with wooden clothespins. On a whim, she took the day off from work. The warm wind lifted her hair to curl around the brim of her beloved hat, whose band contained a circlet of sunflowers. She gazed down the line where her mother played with Matthew on the grass and smiled. Catherine stood and picked up the baby before walking over to a flower patch, and held his chubby arm out to the petals.

"Pretty," she said, and he reached out to yank several beautiful flowers off their stems in a greedy handful. "No, Matty." He gave a maniacal laugh.

Her mother chided his action, in gentle reprimand, as the air shifted. Darkness fell over Dee's vision like a cloud eclipsing the sun. Pain radiated through her core, and she turned toward the patch of flowers she planted under Matt's banyan tree. They bloomed, withered and died, as a howl caused her eyes to shift outward. The ocean and sky blended into monochromatic colors, with a single beam of golden sunlight piercing the darkening cloud. It spotlighted a place on the ocean, as an evil wind blew over her and rustled the leaves in the old banyan tree. She raised a hand to her décolletage and stumbled back.

Her heart raced as an intense burning sensation bled down into her gut, then the weight of the world sat down on her chest. *Heart attack?* She closed her eyes and allowed a sensation of air bubbles in her blood to move through her. Her stomach dropped, as if falling from a skyscraper, and Arthur came to her in a vision behind her closed eyelids. A light flickered in her heart, then extinguished. When Dee opened her eyes again an enormous water funnel spun around the beam of sunlight causing Dee to fall to her knees. She blinked, and it vanished.

Trying to regain some composure, she glanced over at her mother who also observed the sea, her expression mirroring her daughters. *Did Mama see it too?* Dee opened her mouth to ask, when the doorbell chimed inside the house, and the two women locked eyes, knowing. Standing on shaking legs, Dee moved through her home and opened the front door.

On the stoop stood her former boss, Bert Norton, Maleko Ho, and beside him, Evie, who's eyes were red and swollen half shut from crying. A man with a white clergy collar at his throat also stood on the path, a short way away, head bowed. She let out an explosive breath, like someone punched her hard in the stomach, and it forced her to take a step backward.

"Dee." Norton reached out a hand to her. "May I speak with you for a moment inside?"

"No," she snapped back. "Arthur will be home soon, and we're going to the movies. So, I-I have to get ready now." Her chin quivered as she spoke, as Catherine walked around the corner holding Matthew who, sensing his mother's distress, whimpered.

"Honey, it's about Arthur," Maleko said, and only then did she take in his overalls and shirt, covered in a rusty-brown stain. She released a noise in her throat that didn't sound human.

Bert's eyes snapped over to Catherine's, then back at her, as Maleko stepped closer and Evie ran around him to embrace her. Numb detachment settled over Dee, while they described the catastrophic accident that ended her husband's life.

Her mind leapt in fits and starts, as she tried to take in greedy gasps of air. Images beat around her, along with her jack-hammering heartbeat. Norton talking… Mama's hand raised to her mouth… Maleko's sturdy arms around her, pressing Arthur's blood into her own clothes and brilliant blue eyes staring without seeing at the summer sky. Her legs buckled, and Maleko guided her to the floor. Catherine knelt in front of her holding her son, his face reddened with furious tears.

After a time, the sound of her baby's cries brought her back to reality, and she reached for him. Catherine placed him in Dee's arms, tears tracing a path down her own face, then wrapped her own arms around her daughter and grandson.

The men spoke words of farewell, but sounded like buzzing bees, loud and intrusive. Inside, something shattered. The carefree girl and life she lived now irrevocably altered. *I will never laugh with Arthur again.*

Dee stood on the Makawehi bluff. Tears poured from her into the ocean, causing the water to rise and her body to weaken. At a noise, she turned and a cloaked figure approached. The morning mist billowed and thickened around the entity, causing smoky black tendrils of evil to appear from under his robe and extend out in all directions. He lifted the hood from his head and laid it back, as long, bony, and sunken fingers glided down the sash, as if stroking a lover's flesh. Dee blinked and found it hard to draw in air. The being raised a fist, clenching it tight, which caused even less air to enter her lungs, and their eyes connected. She should know this man... This evil... for his presence meant death. Her eyes filled with blood from microscopic hemorrhages erupting behind the sclera.

A brilliant light, brighter than the sun, burned holes in the darkness, yet held no warmth. The mist snapped and crackled against it like a force field, and the most beautiful woman solidified behind it. A metallic liquid pooled in the orbital hollows until it formed a band around her eyes. The ethereal being raised a hand and the dark smoke of evil that continued to surround the area turned on the man, encircling his wrists and ankles, causing him to give an almighty bellow like a wounded animal and vanish.

Breath exploded back into Dee's lungs and she fell onto her hands and knees, panting. When she could lift her head again, the woman exploded into a million mercurial beads and disappeared.

Dee gasped and sprang up from her mattress, soaking wet and shaking. Sobbing, she spun around her room, but discovered it empty. Arthur's side of the bed remained made, and pajamas folded neatly on the chair next to her hat from the previous morning. She lifted a hand to her heaving chest, trying to quiet it, and gazed at the eerie pearlized glare from the clock on her nightstand. It revealed only an hour, and a half passed. She stood on shaking legs and walked to the chair to retrieve her husband's pajamas. She clutched them to her bosom before sitting back down on the chair and staring out at the moonlight, knowing she wouldn't sleep again that night.

The next week blurred into decisions, visitors, and foil-wrapped casseroles. Emotions ran high when Dee demanded to see Arthur at the funeral home. Maleko and Issac told her it would be far better to remember him the way he looked that last morning in their bedroom, rather than the broken shell left behind. It wasn't until Evie asked her if Arthur would want her to look at him that way, that Dee agreed, finally, and collapsed into her arms in renewed sobs.

The new widow walked the house at all hours of the night, no matter how hard Catherine tried to coax her to rest. The morning of Arthur's funeral she stared down at her lost little girl, who succumbed to just a few hours of slumber. Her face pale, eyes bruised and puffy, and her body shrunken and frail, the young woman appeared as vulnerable as a shattered China doll. Hundreds of bundled up tissues surrounded her on the bed and floor, and Catherine almost changed her mind about rousing her.

"Dee, sweetheart?" she whispered, and brushed back her hair. "It's time to wake up, honey."

As the widow woke, the anguish of reality penetrated her consciousness once more, and it broke her mother's heart. Dee blinked, and her eyes focused.

"Mama?" she croaked in a voice foreign to both their ears. "Where's Matty?"

"He's still sleeping, lovie. I just wanted to come in and give you a chance to wake up, maybe take a bath and relax a little, before we go. I don't want you rushing all around this morning. What do you think?" Catherine sat on the edge of the bed and stroked Dee's damp hair, smiling. "If you'd rather sleep that's fine, I just… I remember… Honey, just put one foot on the floor, then the other and try to breathe. You don't have to do anything else."

"Is that what you did?" Dee rolled onto her back, and flung an arm across her forehead, as she stared at the ceiling with a vacant expression.

"Yes," Catherine admitted. "It will feel impossible. There will be days you'll miss him so much you can't breathe, then the next day you might hate him for leaving you and Matty." She tucked several strands of hair behind her daughter's ear. "It'll crush your soul sometimes that he can't be here to watch Matthew grow, and then… it will get a little better and you'll remember some happy times. The wonderful memories will cover up the sharpest points of the pain, and you'll go back and forth between all those emotions for a very long time, but honey," she knelt and tilted Dee's head to look at her, "you will somehow find the strength and get through it, because it's what Arthur would want, what Matthew needs, and it's what you, my darling girl, deserve."

Dee nodded as two fat tears escaped and slid down her face. Catherine kissed her forehead. "So, have yourself a nice hot bath, and try to relax a little, then I thought a little Chamomile tea or orange juice and some toast, unless you'd like something heavier?"

"I'm not hungry at all, Mama."

"I know, but it's going to be a very long and exhausting day, and you need some energy for it, even if it's just a little."

"Okay," Dee agreed resigned, and it twisted her mother's heart to see the fight in her headstrong daughter gone. She kissed her forehead again before standing.

"And don't worry about Matty, I've got him. Just take your time and I'll have breakfast ready whenever you are."

After her mother left, Dee sat on the bed for a long moment, thinking about the day to come, then directed her gaze to the closet. Standing, she padded over to it and opened the louvered doors, revealing her wardrobe. She didn't own a thing with appropriate reverence, and the bright colors stared back at her in lewd accusation. In a cruel twist of irony, she now lived in a black, dark world.

Looking over at the chair next to her bed, Dee discovered the new hat Arthur gave to her on Mother's Day, with all the love in his heart. Sunlight split in rays through the blinds, displacing dust motes only to return to the object sitting on the cushioned seat. The sweet decay of the dead flowers wreathed around its crown perfumed the room. Wanting to preserve the time when her husband lived, she hadn't worn it since his death. Now, she walked over and picked it up from its resting place, then sat down on their bed holding it, dejected.

The tissues mocked her, and she realized she hadn't changed their sheets either, just trying to keep his essence around her a little while longer. More tears escaped from her eyes and rolled down cheeks that lost their bloom until hovering on the tip of her nose. *How can someone's body contain so many tears within it?*

She studied their wedding photo on the wall. She'd chosen light magenta for her dress, not white, to her mother's chagrin. The two women argued over the choice, but Dee informed her mother one could still be a virgin and wear magenta, and anyone that didn't agree could suck on it. However, only when Dee revealed Arthur said she brought the color into a black and white world, did Catherine relinquish control. Closing her eyes, his face manifested, and his voice echoed in her ears.

Be a butterfly, my sassy dove.

Dee directed her gaze at the faded but still somewhat hopeful butterfly on her hat, then over at the closet, thinking of her mother's earlier words about what life would bring next. Not only would her husband disapprove of self-pity, he'd hate it if she lived her life in the fragmented shards of their shattered happily ever after.

Walking over to her closet again, Dee sorted through her clothes. Near the back hung a muumuu

Arthur gave her one Christmas. Its base colors, hot pink, cobalt blue, and lime green, with orange, yellow and purple petaling out from the various flowers. The garment, the brightest thing she owned by far, caused her mouth to quiver into a smile. She'd worn it the day she informed her shell-shocked husband of her pregnancy. Whipping her head back to the discarded hat that laid on Arthur's side of the bed, Dee embraced a new resolve.

Moving the hat to her dresser, she stripped the bed of its sheets, taking a moment to bring Arthur's pillow to her face. The spicy scent of his favorite cologne, Old Spice, lingered there. Drawing in a fortifying breath through her nostrils, she remade the bed with the fresh linens she'd hung on the line, the day he died, and dribbled some of the cologne on the sheets. Giving a nod, she laid her dress down upon the bright sunny coverlet.

As the sheets churned down into the washing machine, Dee walked past her surprised mother and out into the garden. The air, heavy with sun, sand, and ocean, also held the barest hint of suntan lotion, reminding Dee that life continued to creep on, despite her personal agony.

Holding her hat upside down in front of her, she collected the items needed, then retreated to her bedroom, where she assembled a colorful wreath around the headwear's brim. She finished it with a small posy of sugar cubes, before satisfaction prevailed, and she walked into the bathroom to draw a scalding bath. Pouring plumeria bath gel into the water, then fingering in some of the real doughy petals from her garden, she pursed her lips, and a tiny spark of life ignited deep within her. Stripping off the clothes she'd worn for days, then stepping into the hot water, Dee closed her eyes, and allowed only Arthur to fill her mind, her fortification for the hours to come.

The day, though arduous, illustrated the love and friendship of so many people Dee couldn't help but celebrate the life of her husband. After every one left, Bert Norton spoke in quiet undertones to her mother, as they brought the house back to rights. Dee read a story to Matthew and kissed him goodnight before going out to the backyard and listening to the peaceful waves crash against the shore. She heard the slide of the back door and assumed her mother came to check on her.

"I'm okay, Mama." A glass of red wine appeared over her shoulder. The face above hers looked old and worn out, and she sat up in the Adirondack chair.

"Mr. Norton?" Dee's eyes widened. "Sorry, I thought you were Mama."

"Hi, Dee. Can I speak with you for a minute?"

"Sure." She gestured to the other chair and sipped the proffered wine as he settled into it. Bert slugged back a healthy gulp of his whiskey, and Dee turned up a corner of her mouth. "Ya need some liquid courage there, Mr. Norton?"

"Please, call me, Bert." Nonplussed, Norton took a deep breath, releasing it on a sigh. "And yes, I sure do." He gave her a shy smile which she returned.

"Bert, huh?"

He dipped his head, then gazed around the large, picturesque and fragrant landscape of her gardens. Hundreds of colorful birds of paradise flowered across an extensive section of land, about to take flight. Elusive Hawai'ian gardenias, with their aromatic alabaster petals, opened in lucky stars. Blue ginger, hibiscus and every shade of plumeria covered an even larger area, while the various greens of the 'Uki 'Uki covered the ground, along with Moa ferns and Pili grass. In the middle stood the immense banyan tree, its roots waving out along the lush grass, and standing like an ancient warrior for those daring to trespass onto the white sandy beach of the South Pacific.

"This really is a magnificent work of art," he commented with nervous agitation. "I've never been able to keep a bouquet of daisies alive, let alone plants in my backyard. I'm in continued awe of you and your mother's talents." He turned to look at his former employee. "Amazing."

"Thank you," she said with pride, but also wariness. "What's on your mind then, Bert?"

"Well, Dee… I have to admit I don't know how to approach this." He turned to face her. "Please know, I'm not trying to imply anything by this at all. I genuinely liked Arthur. He was a fantastic employee and a terrific man."

"Yes, he was… the best of men," Dee agreed, and sipped her wine. "Thank you."

"Like I said, foremost, I just want to express how sorry I am that this happened and find out how all of you are doing."

"We're doing… Well, I guess we're doing the best we can."

"And money-wise? Today was lovely, but I'm sure it was a heavy burden on top of everything else?"

"We're doing okay, Bert. Thank you… really."

"Okay." He sipped a little more of his whiskey. "The second reason I waited to come out here and talk with you was to see what your intentions might be?"

"My intentions?"

"Yes. Maybe this isn't the right time. Christ," he sipped his drink again. "Truthfully, I don't have a clue when the *right* time is, but…"

"It's okay. I'm not going to take offense… promise."

"Okay. Have you given much thought on what you plan to do now that Arthur's gone? Or… maybe you haven't even gotten that far yet?" He paused, searching for the right words. "How… how angry are you with us, honey?"

Surprised, Dee gazed out at the ocean, but understood the question behind the question. Miscommunication and recklessness killed her husband. The man driving hadn't crushed Arthur on purpose, but his ineptitude… perhaps less harried or rushed, Arthur might still be alive. It had not escaped her ears or notice throughout the day, people whispering behind hands about the man, who now lived at the bottom of a bottle. They also discussed whether she'd sue the company for her husband's death. In truth, she'd spent no time at all considering it yet. After all, it wouldn't bring back him back to her.

Dee glanced back over at her former employer after several minutes. "I don't want to destroy your company, Mr. Norton. You've always been good to Mama and me, *and* Arthur. That being said, my husband's gone. I'm only twenty-five years old and I've got a one-year-old little boy to raise on my own. It's gonna get a lot harder as the years go on. So, I haven't decided on what to do yet."

"I understand. We all go way back, and I think you've always known how I feel about you personally. You've always been a bright spot when I needed it most." Dee smiled and nodded her head. "Truth is, we'll never be able to make up the loss of Arthur, but I *do* want to take care of you, and little Matthew in there, as best as I can and not have to take this thing to court." She stared out at the water. "Dee, I want to offer you sixty thousand dollars from Sugar Grove Plantation and reimburse you the expenses of his funeral." The widow's gaze darted back to him. Norton's eyes drooped, and he looked ancient, as if he hadn't slept in days. "I *know* this can't replace him. I know it can't. It would only be his wages for the next seventeen years, plus some interest on top of it. It could help a little until Matthew turns eighteen." He leaned forward in the chair. "Dee, I've got hundreds of families relying on me and the company, to provide them all a living. I know you could take us to court and probably get a lot more…"

"Bert," Dee held up a hand. "Sixty thousand dollars sounds fair. I don't want to take anything away from anyone else, and I have no interest in going to court either. I can sign something or you can take my word for it."

"Well," he said with a nervous chuckle. "You've never given me any reason to doubt your word, before." He extended a hand, and she shook it. Somewhat relieved, Bert looked out toward the ocean, his old eyes glassy. "Honey, it goes without saying, but if you, Catherine or later on, your boy, ever need a job, or anything, you know where to come. I truly, truly mean that. I thought the world of Arthur." His voice broke, and he cleared his throat, pausing only another moment before saying, "And I'm gonna miss him. So, if I can help you out in any way…"

Dee let her eyes travel back out to the ocean for a brief minute, then her gardens, and waited for regret in the deal to come. It didn't, and she too breathed a sigh of relief.

CHAPTER 5

MARCH 1975

As a single mother and primary breadwinner for the family, Dee's life challenged her. Deciding to invest the money given to her by Sugar Grove Plantation, she concentrated on succeeding with her and her mother's salaries alone. The Cornucopia produced more profit than Catherine's floral shop, and given the age difference between the two women, Dee's mother wanted the primary caregiver role of Matthew. It often meant his mother missed out on some of her son's milestones. A problem she tried to rectify in the evenings and on weekends.

Catherine, or Kupuna, as Matthew called her, often indulged the whims of her grandson, taking a more lenient approach to his upbringing than she ever did for Dee, much to her daughter's chagrin. At times, the repeated coddling and lack of discipline created its own problems, and Dee needed to inject frequent doses of reality into the boy's routine. It caused their relationship to fray, and disagreements to occur between her mother and herself about his rearing.

"What does your mom say when you confront her about it?" Evie asked as they tore down the St. Patrick's Day décor in favor of Easter tidings. She ran a strip of tape over a box to seal the contents shut.

"Well, at five when he threw tantrums in stores because he didn't get what he wanted, she said, all kids act that way." Dee labeled the box and stacked it. "When he was seven and used a marker to destroy all the Father's Day projects in his class…"

"Oh, God, I remember that." Evie picked up a green crystal leprechaun hat and wrapped it in paper.

"She said, the boy lost his father, and he missed him." Dee finished taping the bottom of another box and set it on the table. "I told her I missed Arthur too, but didn't stop others from kissing each other in public because of it."

"What did she say when you said that?" Evie reached for some bubble-wrap.

"She got pissed. Last year, he got in a fight with a kid and pulled out a chunk of his hair."

"Wait." Evie stopped wrapping the hat and looked at her friend in disbelief. "When was that? You didn't tell me anything."

"Beginning of the school year." Dee picked up her coffee and sipped from it. "Mama refused to believe it was malicious and said the other boy started it." She switched to a slight falsetto. "Matt was just protecting himself, Deidre."

"Naturally, what's he supposed to do against a bully?" Evie said with sarcasm.

"Yeah, except no one tells you what to do when your kid's the bully." Dee sighed. "The problem is, I know he misses Arthur, or at least the idea of Arthur. Ya know a man?"

"Do you? Miss having a man, I mean?"

"God, Eve, I don't even know anymore."

Evie set the crystal into the box, grabbed her coffee, then turned to her friend. "Maybe it's time to try again, Dee. You know it would be okay to do so. Arthur would want you to be happy."

"I know. I'm just so tired all the time." Dee finished taping the next box and labeled it, before taking up her mug and sipping. "I don't feel like I have an ounce of energy for one more thing. Plus, what's the point? I had perfection, that kind of thing comes around once in a lifetime."

"No, it doesn't."

"Yes… it does. You can come close but the circumstances… the way I was back then versus now… I'm a different person now, Evie." She grabbed another box and taped the bottom. "Matty still has those horrible nightmares when he says he's drowning and monsters and demons are after him. The extra time I have needs to go to him right now."

"Maybe you guys should go back to counseling. It seemed to help before."

"Not according to Mama." The bell chimed over the door at the same time the phone rang. "You help them. I'll get the phone." Evie reached out and squeezed her hand as Dee picked up the receiver. "Dee's Cornucopia, this is Dee."

Tucker Patterson, a mere slip of a boy, ran from the second-grade classrooms to the swings with a bunch of his friends in tow. Matthew followed him with his eyes, scowling. The group commandeered the swing set and began a contest of who could swing higher. Dee's son darted a gaze at his own friends and sneered. *All they do is talk about boring stuff. They never want to do anything fun.* Tucker not only had better friends, but he also had a Fundae Friday, or ice cream pop covered in a hard chocolate shell for those who paid for it. Matt lost his Fundae Friday for a month, because he back-talked his mother, and jealousy fanned into flame as he observed the youngsters play and giggle, not requiring *his* presence at all. Face burning crimson, he advanced on the small group.

"Get off that, now," Matthew demanded.

"Nuh-uh, I just got on the swing," Tucker replied, giggling.

"I said off. I want to swing now."

"So."

"So, I'm bigger than you."

"You aren't the boss of me," Tucker declared with a taunting edge, and stuck out his tongue. Remembering his ice cream just before it fell off the stick, he took a quick bite, then threw it toward his new nemesis.

"Get off!"

"No!" the boy screamed and pumped his legs harder.

Uncontrolled rage bubbled over inside Matthew and he grabbed one of the child's legs and yanked. The second-grader jerked out of the seat and fell hard, banging his head onto the ground. Tucker's eyes squeezed together as he curved into a fetal position and held his head. He opened his mouth like a tragedy mask, about to unleash a blood-curdling shriek, and Matthew grabbed the ice cream that fell on the playground floor. Several wood chips, meant to soften the earthen floor, stuck to the sticky treat and Matt crammed it all into the little boy's mouth, to muffle the oncoming wail, then ran away.

Dee slammed the front door so hard the windows rattled. "George Matthew Taylor! Where the hell are you!" She rounded the corner to the surprised expressions of her mother at the kitchen stove and her son watching television. *At least, the boy has the excellent sense to look guilty.*

"Dee?"

"Were you going to tell me, Mama?" Dee swung around to face Catherine. "Were you going to tell me he beat up a kid three years younger than him?"

"He didn't beat him up," her mother said sardonically. "The boy fell off the swing and landed on the ground, then got embarrassed and said Matty did it."

"Is that right?" Dee retorted, almost song-like. "That's funny, because a lot of other kids *and* the playground lady saw it differently." Her head snapped to her child and spoke through gritted teeth. "Turn that TV off right now and get your ass in here, young man."

"Deidre!"

"What?" Dee spat back. "That little boy is in second grade, Mama. Second grade! And a lot smaller than Matthew. You can't keep defending this behavior." She studied her son. "What do you have to say for yourself?"

"I didn't push him," Matthew lamented, afraid of his mother's angry face.

"An entire playground watched you pulled him down and then shove a bunch of wood chips in his mouth. You realized he could've choked to death?"

"Dee, you are blowing this way out of proportion."

She ignored her mother and waited out her son. Seeing his usual tactics weren't working, Matthew shrugged, then blurted, "They didn't tell you he was being mean, Mom. He was being really mean to me first."

"Bullshit!"

"Deidre…"

"Mother! Stop it!" She refocused her attention on her son.

"It was a bad day, and I missed Daddy." Tears welled up in his eyes.

"Oh, no you don't," Dee scolded. "That excuse doesn't work on me. Your father died eight years ago. I know it's hard. It's been a damn sight hard on all of us, but we do not use it as an excuse to hurt other people." The boy stared down at his feet in an angry pout. "George Matthew, look at me!"

He did, but rather than look contrite, he appeared more concerned that his words fell on deaf ears.

"Your father was the best man I ever knew. He was good and kind and hardworking. That's what *he* was all about. Like me, he'd so disappointed in your decisions today. Picking on someone younger and weaker than yourself." The tears rolled over the rims of her son's vivid eyes, which held the same unworldly quality as Arthur's. "I know that isn't a pleasant thing to hear, and it sure as hell isn't a pleasant thing to say, but it's the plain truth. And this behavior of acting up, whining, screaming, and beating kids up is gonna stop right now. Do you understand me, son?" She gave him a small shake. "Do you hear me?"

"Deidre," Catherine whispered as her grandson cried. "He's at an age when his father's approval would mean everything to him. How can you be so…?" Her words trailed off as Matthew ran to his grandmother and pillowed his head on her bosom, and her daughter's gimlet stare turned toward her.

"He's hurting the other children in school because they aren't paying enough attention to him, Mama," Dee said eyeing her son. "It will stop, and it'll stop right now."

"Why do you even care?" Matthew yelled, peeking out from Catherine's apron. "You can't tell me what to do! You can't touch me!"

"Oh yeah," Dee retorted almost in a chuckle, and advanced on him, her eyes widening. "Say another word out of turn, boy, just one more and I'll blister your ass for you. You won't be able to sit down for a week."

"Enough!" Catherine exclaimed. "No one's touching anyone."

Authority undermined once more, Dee whipped her head toward her mother.

"No, Mama. I understand you're trying to help, and you've been an absolute Godsend to me, but I have to do this for Matty's sake. I also understand if you don't want to take care of him anymore because of what's about to happen, but we need to try something different now. If you can't follow *my* rules on how he should be raised, then let me know now and I'll make other arrangements. We can even move into the shop."

"What are you talking about?"

"Matthew, sit down." Dee reached into her bag and withdrew a sheet of paper. She stared at her mother and said, "If you're onboard than sit down, Mama. If not, could you please give us a minute?" Without knowing what to say, Catherine sat, and losing his refuge, Matt sat too.

"Number one, the school has suspended you for a week, but that doesn't mean you'll sit on your ass and watch TV all day. Tonight, you'll write a letter to Tucker, apologizing for what you did to him." Matthew drew his brows together and his mouth formed a perfect O. "It will be sincere, and you'll make sure he knows it will *never* happen again. Then you'll write another letter to your school about how wrong it is to bully. After that, you can go to your room where you can read or play with your toys until seven, when you will go to bed." Matthew gasped.

"But..." She raised a hand.

"Tomorrow you'll come with me and deliver both those letters to the front office, and you'll tell Tucker you're sorry in person and you'll read your other letter over the school intercom." Matthew's lower lip trembled.

"Mom… No!"

"Oh yes," she retorted. "I've arranged for them to give you all your homework for the week, so you don't fall behind. Every morning you'll get up at regular time, do your homework and the list of chores *I* give you, with no help from Kupuna." Dee's gaze snapped up to her mother, who stared back at her with a look she couldn't read. Dee glanced down at her notes again and read on. "On Tuesday and Thursday, you're going back to Dr. Williams, the counselor."

"Why? He's stupid," Matthew complained.

"It didn't help all that much before," her mother added.

"Because you keep talking about how much you miss Daddy, and if that's true, you need to work through those feelings." Dee observed her son, who blanched like someone caught him in a lie, and now he faced his penance.

"I don't miss him a lot, just sometimes."

"Yes, I know that, but it's also difficult having me for a mom. I wear funny clothes, I got a big mouth, and I work long hours." She ran a hand through her hair. "I've let things spin out of control here and you know what?"

"What?"

"Daddy would be very disappointed in some of my decisions too." She placed a hand on his shoulder and reached the other to clasp her mother's hand. "The three people at this table are all I care about, and if we're going to make it, we have to work together." She squeezed, then looked down at the table. "Now, go to your room and get started on those letters." Her son gave a pleading look toward his Kupuna and a fulminating one to his mother before rising from the table, stomping into his room, and slamming the door.

Dee walked over to the counter and poured her mother and herself a glass of wine. She handed one to Catherine.

"Come on, Mama, let's go outside a minute." Without waiting for an answer, she slid open the patio door and walked out as day gave way to twilight. Her mother followed, and they sat in the humid night air, listening to the ocean for a long time. The banyan tree stood sentinel but pulsed with power, seeping into Dee's circadian rhythm, just as it always did when she came near it. Her mother paused, looked up into its branches and smiled as if addressing a friend, before her face slipped back into a mask of frustrated resolution, and both women faced each other.

"Mama, I'm sorry," Dee murmured. "I know you're angry with me."

"It's not that I'm angry, I just think you're being too harsh. He's only a boy, Deidre, a baby. And I don't appreciate you criticizing my ability to take care of him. I was a parent long before you, you know, and you didn't turn out too bad."

"That's just it, Mama, he's *not* a baby anymore. He'll be ten-years-old in three months," Dee retorted. "In another ten years he'll be grown-ass man. I don't think I'm being harsh at all. He's completely out of control." She sipped her wine, before adding, "And I didn't turn out so bad because you would've beaten my butt if I did half of what he's done. I mean, you let me be me, and that was great, but Matthew's different. He takes advantage of that generosity and needs a smack upside the head now and again, or life's not gonna turn out that well for him." She reached out a hand to her mother. "Please, Mama, do this with me. We've got to be united, or he'll play us against each other. Plus," Dee paused and sighed. "I'm *always* the bad guy. If Arthur were here, we'd be splitting that chore and I'd have some support." Catherine's hand stiffened. "Please, Mama… I don't want him to hate me. He's all I got left of Arthur."

Her mother's eyes softened, and she lowered a chastened head before uttering, "Okay. I'll try to respect your wishes." She darted a glance toward her daughter.

"But, I am his Kupunawahine, not his mother, and I have a right to spoil him some, too."

"You're right. Don't think I don't know or appreciate what you've done for me and for us."

"It isn't a chore, honey, and you're right, we're in this together. I'll try hard. I promise, okay?"

"Okay." Dee sipped her wine and stared out at the darkness. "The rest we'll deal with as it comes."

CHAPTER 6

AUGUST 1976

FRESH FROM HER YEARLY girls' weekend getaway with Evie, Dee leaned on her rake to rest and looked around her small empire. In the fourteen years since she first opened the Cornucopia's doors, she created an Eden. Her sense of pride in what she made, with only a ninth-grade education, baffled but also inspired her to grow, learn and become even better. Matt still experienced nightmares and occasionally made poor choices, but he seemed less angry. It caused Dee to smile.

"Hey, Dee." She snapped out of her daydream and looked over at Evie. "You got a call from your mom. I think she needs some help."

"Okay, I'll take it in the office." She quickly washed her hands in the outside sink and ran to the small bedroom she'd turned into an office for herself. Snatching up the receiver, she said breathlessly, "Hey, Mama. Everything okay?"

"Dee! There's water everywhere! I think something's wrong with the sink again."

"Okay," Dee sighed. "Well, turn the water off under the cabinet then, and I'll take a look when I get home."

"This place is just falling apart!" her mother exclaimed. "We still gotta fix the back-bathroom toilet. Both the car and the truck are leaking oil and… and…"

"All right, Mama," Dee said wearily. "I'll arrange for someone to cover and get everything fixed this weekend okay?"

"Okay, well, we need to get all of Matthew's school supplies and school clothes too. Not to mention some groceries. It's Friday, Dee, can't you come home early tonight? I wanted to go to dinner with Gert and Millie at six."

Dee glanced at the stacks of invoices and bills on her desk and sighed. Not wanting to deny her mother the same break she'd just received, she agreed to come home. She collected her things and stuffed them into her patchwork bag.

"Eve," she said, closing the door and walking up to the checkout station. "I gotta go early. Mama's having a hissy fit. Can you close up?"

"Sure. Go get 'em tiger." Dee raised a fist in the air as if exclaiming, *I will prevail,* and drove home.

By the next morning, she'd burned through most of her honey-do list with just a few items left to complete. Sweat trickled down between her breasts from the humid day, and she lifted her hat off her long blonde hair.

"Mama?"

"In here," Catherine called from the laundry room.

"Hey." Dee swung around the doorjamb, breathless. "Have you seen the indoor tool kit? I'm trying to put together that computer table, and I need a Phillip's screwdriver."

"Whatever that is." Her mother smiled, snapped a towel down, and folded it, thinking. "Why don't you look in the back of my closet."

"Anywhere specific?"

"Maybe behind the suitcases."

"Thanks."

After she retrieved the tool and moved to replace the bags, her peripheral vision caught a reflection off some metal high on the closet shelf. A box she'd never seen before sat amongst her mother's belongings.

Perplexed, she reached up and seized the heavy object, then sat cross-legged on the floor, tucking her kaleidoscope skirt around her, before studying the box. Power throbbed from a deep carving, etched upon the lid's surface of old wood, making it feel alive.

Metal straps boasted an ancient worn patina, with medieval rivets dotting along its edges. Dee turned it over, drawing her brows together at the scent of ambrosia. *How do I know that? What the hell is ambrosia?* There didn't seem to be a latch or any way to open it and, aside from the carving, nothing else marred its surface. Uncertain, she turned the container over again and studied the coat of arms, as her fingers glided across the grooved surface.

A large standard, gold-rimmed shield, with golden wings and swirls on either side of it. Two pitchforks or tridents, each with three prongs, stuck out of the top at opposite angles. A strong pull claimed her focus to the left one where the center tine extended further out from the other two. She ran her index finger along the groove and her heart skipped a beat. She stared a moment longer, then let her gaze run to the right trident's center prong protruding just below the other two. Between them lay a cornucopia bursting with a colorful bounty of fruits and vegetables, much like the one carved on the sign outside her shop. A lovely dove, its talons up, as if about to perch atop the abundance, opened its wings wide. In wonderment, Dee's fingers ran over the shield, divided into four sections.

The upper left background, stained a deep Persian blue, contained two interlocking gold rings and a silver… Dee peered closer… *is that an old-time anvil?* The right upper quadrant's background, stained black, contained a large white lyre. Butterflies exploded into the young widow's belly, almost like life itself. After a moment, her eyes shifted on the lower right quadrant. Again, it contained the same Persian blue backdrop as the upper left, but within it lay an archaic goblet or chalice. A bow and arrow hovered above it, cocked and ready to fire from the quiver. Her gaze darted to the last quadrant that contained a snowy white barn owl, eyes focused on her, and stark against the black background. At the base of the shield, flames licked up toward the sky, and where the four quadrants joined in the center, a large pearly orb and huge black thunderbolt seared through the middle, connecting them all.

"I've been wondering when I should give that to you."

Dee gave a violent start and whipped her head around. Breathless, Catherine stood in the doorway, silver hair unbound and loose upon her shoulders, her skin more rounded and youthful somehow.

"What *is* this, Mama?" Dee resumed her focus back on the box.

"Well, to be honest, I'm not sure." Catherine walked over to the bed and sat down. "My mother gave it to me a long time ago, before she died and just said we've handed it down for generations." She drew her brows together as she peered at it. "It's part of our history, so I kept it for you." Dee could feel her mother's eyes on her. "Did you think you were the only one in the family that could sense things?"

In fact, the young woman *did* believe that. Box forgotten, she gazed at her matriarch, taking in her creamy skin and rather uncharacteristically bright blue eyes.

"You saw the water that day too, didn't you?"

"The day Arthur died?"

"Yes. I looked over at you and thought you saw it too, but we never talked about it."

"See what?"

"Come on, Mama."

"All right, yes, I saw the water and the sunlight but… I don't know." She studied her long fingers, then wrung her hands together. "I don't think I have the sight as much as you do. At least not anymore. Or maybe mine is just different. I don't get the visions that accompany yours sometimes. My kupunawahine did, though."

"Why didn't you tell me that? Do you feel the banyan tree too?"

"Well," Catherine chuckled and ignored her last question in favor of her first. "I'm not sure what to tell. My Kupuna never told me much about her gift, just that she had it." Catherine's eyes couldn't stay connected with her daughter's and scurried away. She stood and went to the window, staring out at the old banyan, its roots growing up from the earth into the massive branches of its magnificent canopy. "When you started having the aptitude… Well, you were so little, I didn't know how to help you with it and she'd already passed on by then. It didn't seem to hurt anything, so I let it be."

"So, you believe me… that I have it?"

Her mother laughed out loud. "Well, of course I do. I never doubted it, honey, and always thought you were fearless in the way you embraced it. It's the thing I admire most about you. I never… you're so brave, Deidre." The woman walked back to her daughter, laid her hands on the crown of her head, leaned down and kissed her hair. "Anyway." She straightened, and cleared her throat, before gesturing to the box, "I've been meaning to give that to you for some time now. So, why don't you go put it away and give me a hand with dinner?"

Dee wanted to ask a million questions but said instead, "Okay, I'll be right there." She walked to her room and found the only available space to store the ancient gift, deep in the recesses of her own closet. She'd find a better place later, but the chest and her interest in it faded, as if someone pulled it from her thoughts on a thread, saving it for another time.

In the wee hours of night, Catherine opened her eyes to a bright, golden light shining through her bedroom window. She sat up, slipped her bare feet into slippers and grabbed the soft chenille bathrobe hanging on her bedpost. Padding over to the window, she searched through the open louvered blinds. A brilliant star west of Jupiter winked back at her.

Preparing herself, she closed her eyes, unlocked the slider and stepped out onto the spongy grass of their backyard. When she opened them again, the massive banyan still stood guard in the waxing moonlight, and she walked to it. As the island slept, she straightened her arms next to her sides. Lifting her arms backward, palms down, she splayed her fingers out and slowly turned her palms up. The warm wind lifted, and as she lifted her arms, the flowers opened and sparked pollen into the air in small puffs.

She peered down at the ground, and a small sunflower seedling sprouted and grew, like a time-lapsed movie, until it hovered several feet above her. Its bright sunny face bobbed down, and the seeds within it glistened as they separated into a soft glowing face. Eyes, the color of bright jade, and framed in lovely, long black lashes, slowly widened and blinked at her. The stalk of the sunflower turned into the cloak-clad body of a woman, as the happy petals curled into golden brown hair down the goddess' back.

Catherine knelt before her, and placed a hand to her heart, tilting her head down. "Kupunawahine," she murmured.

Demeter, Greek goddess of harvest and agriculture, curved her lips into a radiant smile. "Rise, my child."

Catherine stood and gave a shaky smile back at her. "She has found the chest, then?"

"Yes, last night. It took everything I had not to tell her everything." Catherine searched her ancestor's eyes. "How can you expect me to keep this from her?"

"It is not her time. The wheels of fate have turned many times only to fail," Demeter whispered. "Our power has already waned in our dimension. We have spent lifetimes waiting for this moment to arrive. It will begin with your daughter, and nothing will interfere with that."

"I just don't see why you don't tell me, so I can help her. She has the sight, but she doesn't understand how to use it or… any of this." Giving a helpless gesture to her surroundings, her eyes pleaded with the goddess. "She suspects my power, but it feels like it's almost gone now. What's happening?"

"Themis has done what she can to transfer your ability to Deidre," Demeter replied, referring to the Oracle of Delphi. "The last drop of my blood flows within her now and her power will grow with time, as we need it."

"When you first came to me, all those years ago, and said something was coming, I asked you what it was. You said you'd tell me when the time came, but you still haven't." Catherine tried to calm her rising voice and thundering heart.

"Do you know how hard this is? How difficult our lives have been? After George died, and you told me they sacrificed him, along with all the others… Do you have any idea how hard that was to accept? And then you took Arthur… Arthur! I pleaded with you, but you took him anyway… you took them both. They were good men… decent men! How am I supposed to explain that to her? How do I tell her she's descended from a Greek goddess who doesn't give a damn about her life, yet wants her to give up everything for *her* cause? It's selfish and cruel."

"You will disclose nothing," Demeter said with condescension. "The time for her to awaken is not for *you* to say."

"She is *my* daughter," Catherine snapped. "I have every right. This has been a horrible burden to live with. Something you know nothing about."

"Not being able to communicate with my daughter?" Demeter snapped back with vicious disdain. "Yes! I do. You forget yourself, mortal, for Hades stole my own daughter from me. Be thankful we do not take yours away from you. Deidre's purpose is stronger than your own, and we choose her. *You* are expendable."

"Oh, well, thanks for that," Catherine snapped, and tears filled her eyes. "I guess that shouldn't come as a tremendous shock, now should it?"

Demeter's eyes softened. "My child, you have served your purpose and protected the chosen. Her fate and purpose will reveal itself many years from now, as she protects the foundation."

"What does that mean… the foundation? Foundation of what?"

"Not what… who."

"God damn it, stop talking in circles."

"You are not worthy to know."

Catherine stood and poked a stern finger at the goddess. "But I am worthy enough to have a power I didn't understand and pass it down to my daughter."

"You have taught her to accept her place and her power."

"Like hell I have. I don't even know what her place and power are because you won't tell me." She leaned in, her face mere inches from the deity. "I will tell you one thing though, if I don't start getting some answers, I will blow the lid off this whole damned thing. Don't think for a second that I won't. You don't control her or me." She stepped back. "So, you better start revealing shit soon or I promise you, neither one of us will ever lift a finger to help you or any of the others, ever again."

Catherine turned her back on the goddess and stomped back toward the house, closing the sliding door with a bang.

Furious, Demeter waved a hand to soften the noise of the door before it reached anyone's ears and settled the house with her other hand. She gazed up at the bright light in the sky.

"You must deal with this blight, niece," Themis' voice echoed in her mind. "The last drop of blood is nigh upon us. This will be our last chance."

Demeter's face fell at the all-knowing Oracle. "She has been a loyal and faithful servant, perhaps…"

"Demeter, we have all risked, and many more sacrifices are yet to come. Catherine is not Persephone. We must allow the mortals to gain their strength, for no one is yet in place beside Deidre, and even she will not be ready until her hair turns white and her skin becomes lax. Many years in their dimension. It's time for us to prepare, for my father seeks revenge."

Demeter understood what she did not say. If they didn't win this time, no hope remained.

CHAPTER 7

T HE NEXT DAY CATHERINE, exhausted, dropped off Matt at school and drove into town for groceries. She found a grocery cart and leaned on its handle as she walked. Sleeping fitfully after meeting with the goddess, she dreamed of dark things. The wheel jumped and squeaked on the carrier as she tottered down the aisles. Lifting her head to reach for some cereal, a wave of vertigo feathered through her. She closed her eyes against an oily void and gave a shake of her head to clear it. Her face flushed, and perspiration bubbled across her upper lip and temple as she struggled to catch a breath. A boy in his early twenties stocked shelves nearby and glanced down the aisle at her. She reached a hand out to him, pain resonating in her chest.

"Are you all right, ma'am?" The boy ran the last few steps to help her to a sitting position on the floor, then knelt beside her. She expected his touch, but her arm only registered heavy numbness.

"Something's… weird," she panted, and laid her head down on the cool floor. Black ribbons of energy slithered down the sides of the aisle, coming for her, and Catherine's eyes widened.

"Somebody!" the boy yelled. "Somebody help me! Ma'am? Can you hear me?" His feet sent reverberations through the linoleum as he ran for help.

Visions of past dream invaders flashed in and out of her mind. An ancient-looking man with gigantic hands curved around an orb of energy. Three hags with something on their faces. A shadow in the dark, and some willowy, blindfolded woman flinging her hands outward. Power emanated through everything like a tsunami wave. A tall, muscular blond man with a large trident tattoo on his back, like the one on the ancient chest, turned to look back over his shoulder at her. A beautiful woman with a golden lyre opened her mouth to sing, and physical music poured out from her, yet she couldn't understand how. *Music isn't physical.* And then, Dee. Her daughter's youthful face aged to that of an old woman in seconds. The ancient box opened with a bright light pulsating within. *The goddess is showing me what is to come.* An intense pressure pushed down on the old woman's chest and radiated out her shoulders and down her back, as the slithering bands entered her and squeezed around her heart.

"My precious child." Demeter floated into her vision, smiled at her and laid a soothing hand on her forehead. Diamonds popped and sparkled around the perimeter of the scene. "This is not punishment. You have completed your part of the quest. Now rest with your husband in the Elysium."

Terrified, Catherine closed her eyes, and the pain left her body. When she opened them a final time, she had all the knowledge of the world, both in ancient times and modern, and Dee's beautiful laughing face.

"Deidre…" she called out once, the second syllable ending with her exhale, then slipped away into the abyss.

Dee stood in Cornucopia's center garden watering when once again, Evie announced a phone call. Dee smiled and waved, showing she'd take it in her office, and wiped dirty, damp hands off on her smock.

"Hello there, this is Dee."

"Hello, Mrs. Taylor?"

"Yes."

"This is Dr. Rosalie Yonkers over at St. Cecilia General."

Dee's heart skipped a beat. "Is it Matthew, or my mama, Catherine Walker?"

"Yes, ma'am, your mother. They brought her in about an hour ago, with a massive cardiac event."

"Oh God! Is she okay?" Dee searched around her office for her bag and car keys.

"Ma'am, we need for you to…"

"Stop calling me ma'am, damn it!" Dee demanded, patting her pockets. "Is she okay?"

A deep sigh whispered across the line. "No, Mrs. Taylor, I'm sorry, she's not. We exhausted every resource, but there was just so much damage, and we couldn't revive her. She expired ma… ah, Mrs. Taylor, and I'm so very sorry for your loss."

"Ah." Dee squeaked, the sharp jab to her mid-section was like a physical blow. She dropped the receiver on the floor, but could still hear the doctor speaking. Ignoring her, pain settled throughout her body, and she panted through it for several moments.

Mama… gone? She didn't receive even the barest hint of a warning. Her consciousness filled with Catherine, Arthur, and her father in full military dress. Bodies still and voices silent. *How much more can fate take from me?* Matthew solidified next to them, and her heart dropped even more. Arthur's death had been hard enough on the boy, but losing his Kupuna would be catastrophic.

Breathing heavily, Dee glimpsed her keys sitting on her desk and grabbed them. Running past her stunned staff without a word, she drove to the hospital and asked a lady at reception where to go. The elderly lady escorted her through the small hospital to her mother's quiet, dark room. No machines beeped. No procedures performed. Just a small, clean room that contained the small body of the woman she loved most in the world. Catherine laid serenely on the bed with her arms folded atop the crisp sheet.

She stared down at the body with numb detachment. Tears welled in her eyes and dripped down her cheeks and onto her chest. She leaned down to her mother's ear.

"Are you close by? Do you know how much I love you, Mama?" she whispered, but the room remained silent, "Are you here? I love you, so much… Tell Daddy and Arthur, I love them too." Dee exploded into sobs.

After what seemed like days, she glanced up at the clock on the wall and discovered an hour passed. *Waste. Anger.* The emotions rooted and blossomed. *Why?* Receiving no answer, Dee stood, collected her keys and the small bag containing her mother's possessions. She hovered a moment longer, just gazing at her mother's lovely face, then leaned over and kissed her temple. With the hour still early, she walked out into the sunlight.

Though the initial shock devoured her, she recognized the arduous days ahead. Sitting in her car, she tried to think about what to do next, and spent the rest of the afternoon at the local funeral home making plans and getting organized before coming home to gut her child with the horrendous news.

As expected, losing his beloved Kupuna devastated Matthew. His mother leaned against the headboard of her bed and stroked her son's damp hair as his sorrow poured out of him, softened into hiccups, until finally he slept. She stayed an hour more in the darkness, then laid his head on the pillow and padded through the quiet house to Catherine's room. Reaching out a hand, she took a pillow from the bed before trekking out into the night and beautiful backyard sanctuary they'd created together. The waves crashed against the sand as Dee wept out her grief into her mother's pillow. Tricked and forsaken by her gift, she trembled and clenched her fists, eyes accusing the darkness and shadows of the banyan tree.

She tried to gain strength and courage from both her husband and her mother, behind closed lids, but only discovered utter loneliness for the first time in her existence. She still had Matthew, but their lives would once more change, as she tried to solidify the moving parts of what it would look like to move forward.

After a week of planning, preparing, and implementing, Dee sat in the viewing room of the funeral home, in the same outfit she'd buried her husband in. She scanned her mother's face and body, as it laid in the cerulean blue satin of the mahogany coffin. The old woman looked plastic and foreign, but also at peace. Dee's eyes kept trailing to the two stitches holding her mother's eyelids together, and each time they did, her stomach plummeted in nauseous complaint. Sunlight streamed through the stained-glass windows, and she turned her attention to the colorful byplay on the walls and floor. *Mama would've loved that.*

The door squeaked on its hinges, and she glanced over to find Matthew standing in the doorway. He wore his nicest khaki pants, a subdued Hawai'ian shirt and traditional maile and ti leaf lei's. He insisted on hair gel that morning and slicked back his golden locks with respectful maturity. Yet, just now he appeared young, lost and alone.

"Mom?"

"Hi, Matty," Dee wobbled into a smile. "How you doing, baby?" When the boy said nothing, just stared at the coffin, eyes filling with tears, Dee cooed, "Come here, honey."

He ran over to her, buried his face into the curve of her shoulder, and she kissed the top of his head, smelling the thick hair gel and pre-teen boy. During the service, the mortuary's occupants overflowed outdoors, as over a hundred island inhabitants attended Catherine Walker's funeral and luncheon. Now, in the resounding silence, with the long afternoon and evening ahead of them, the mother and son slumped in their chairs.

The door creaked again, and they both looked up to see Evie and Issac standing in the doorway. "You guys need anything?"

"Everyone gone?"

"Yeah, last one just left."

"You guys should take off too, the kids'll be waiting for you." Dee said, referencing the couple's two young children.

"Oh, no, we want to help clean up."

"It's okay, Eve, it's part of the service. Go on home. I'll call you tomorrow and, thank you honey, for everything."

"Okay," Evie replied, still sounding unsure, but Issac gripped her hand and mother and son found themselves alone again.

"Matty?" Dee asked, after a moment, and kissed his head once more. "Let's go to the beach. You want to?"

"What for?"

"A surprise."

"Really?"

"Really. Come on, let's go."

They turned and said their last goodbyes to Catherine, before leaving her forever. An hour later they pulled into Kiahuna Beach. As the boy climbed out and shut the door on their late model sedan, he gave his mother a bewildered look. Dee went to the trunk of the car and retrieved the overnight bag she placed there the night before in preparation.

"Come on," she said, extending her hand out to him. Pausing only for a moment, he slid his hand into hers and they walked down to a small shack on the beach.

A man in his early twenties, with curly, black, shoulder-length hair stepped out of the building. Tall and trim, he wore floral board shorts and a red tee shirt with *Surf's Up Rentals* heat transferred across the chest. He greeted them with a clipboard and a warm smile.

"Aloha!" the cheerful man called out and extended a hand to each of them. "My name's Eric. I'll be your instructor today."

Matthew gaped at his mother while he shook Eric's hand. "Instructor?"

"Yeah," Dee replied, "We're gonna learn how to surf."

"We are? Today?" Her son's face brightened. "Really, Mom?"

"Yep. I thought we could do this together. What do ya think?"

"Okay," he replied with hopeful anticipation.

Dee and Matthew changed from their funeral wear into swimsuits, and Eric further fitted the pair into wetsuits and surfboards. He taught them how to wax the boards down and attach the leashes to their ankles so they wouldn't lose their equipment. The instructor spent the next hour teaching them the finer points of how to pop or jerk up to a standing position with one foot centered in the middle of the board and the other a little more than a hip's distance behind it. After they mastered the initial protocol, he took mother and son out into the water, and they practiced until each caught and rode several waves.

"The more you practice, the faster you'll learn, and get proficient," Eric pronounced. "But I think you're both naturals."

Dee also packed towels and beachwear for after the lesson, and as they dried off and changed, she asked Eric where to go for the best gear. He told her and, to Matthew's surprise, they left to pick out his very own surfboard. She indulged him further when he requested she get one too.

Afterward, they spent the dinner hour roasting hotdogs and marshmallows on the beach just off their house, until the beautiful Hawai'ian sun sizzled into the ocean. Matthew laid on his side in the sand, with his head in his mother's lap.

"I miss Kupuna already," Matthew said, almost to himself.

"Yeah, me too, Matty." Dee stroked his hair. "She would have loved the service and all the people, but it would've thrilled her to know we came and did this, wouldn't it? I don't know why we never did before."

"Cause you're always working."

"I'm sorry."

Her son nodded, eyes glistening. "What's going to happen now?" he asked, not looking up at her. She returned the favor and kept her eyes on the sunset.

"Well, honey, things are going to change. You and me need to work even harder together, to make her proud." She glanced down at him. "We're *still* a family, Matty. That'll never change."

"Will you be home more?"

She realized she would need to be, and in his question understood just how much her absence affected him. "Yes. I still have to make a living, so we can eat and do stuff though."

"And surf."

"And surf, of course." He grinned up at her. "And the summer months will be a little harder with the tourist season, but I'll tell you what." She met his eyes. "I'll try hard to make sure my hours are regular and dependable as much as possible. How about I set up an office at home, and then I can bring all the paperwork and crap back here? What do you think?"

"Yeah, and maybe we can go surfing even more?" He gave the barest hint of a smile. "Eric said we have to practice."

"Absolutely, that's the most fun I've had in ages!"

"Me too." He sat up and hugged her. "I love you, Mom." Tears stung her eyes, as a very long time passed since he last said those three words to her. "Please don't leave me."

"Oh, honey, I'm not going anywhere, are you kidding me? I'm going to be the biggest pain in your ass." He giggled. "And I love you too, Matty." She pressed his head into her shoulder, hugging him tighter. "I want us to talk." She placed her cheek on top of his head. "I want you to tell me when things are bad, okay?"

"Okay," Matthew agreed, and they rocked as the sun disappeared behind Puolo Point.

The next weekend, the duo fulfilled her promise and created a workspace out of Matthew's old bedroom. Since the house contained two master suites, on opposite ends of the house, she asked her son which room he wanted, and the boy chose Catherine's at the front of the house. They re-decorated it to look like a surfer's paradise, complete with a tiki hut canopy, and a surfboard sided bed frame. Dee hoped that maybe, just maybe, they'd make it through to the other side.

CHAPTER 8

THE SUMMER OF MATTHEW'S thirteenth birthday, the island hummed with visitors, and Dee's work hours lengthened to keep up. Matt spent most of his days working odd jobs at the Cornucopia to earn spending money. However, halfway through summer he spent more time at the beach near their home. For long hours, he and his friends surfed, swam, and admired the opposite sex. Grown three inches taller than his mother, he tested his independence and place in the world.

Wading out of the water on a rare occasion alone, he carried his surfboard under an arm in the late afternoon and scanned the area. The beach seemed lonely as tourists and locals deserted it for the evening's entertainment. He laid his board in the sand a few yards away from a tan, shirtless boy. Three or four years older than Matt, the muscular youth with warm golden eyes raised a mashed up looking cigarette to his mouth and inhaled.

"What's up, little man?" The boy asked, as if he swallowed each word, and gave a nod of his head, holding the smoke in his lungs. He let it out in a hard exhale. "Wanna hit?"

Matthew peered at the cigarette and Dee's warnings exploded in his head like cannon fire. "I've never smoked a cigarette before."

"It's not a fucking cigarette, you idiot," the kid retorted with disgust. "It's a joint." He sniffed. "You know… pot."

"Oh."

"I 'spose you've never done that before neither?" The boy chuckled and took another drag. "Never mind." He stood, and brushed the sand off his board shorts, yawned, then padded across the beach.

"Wait." Matthew took a few steps toward him. "What do I have to do?"

The kid smiled, sniffed again, and extended a hand, holding out the drug. "Ya just inhale and hold it in as long as you can, before you blow it out."

"Okay." Matt took the proffered joint and pressed it between trembling lips. He drew in the smoke but held it in his mouth.

"No, no, no." The kid moved to him and grabbed the joint from between his fingers. "Take a deep breath and hold it in your lungs." Matthew took a lungful of air and held it. "Right, now do that with the smoke, man."

He tried and at first, nothing. The second try elicited a burning sensation in his lungs, causing them to spasm and him to cough. Something that tasted like dirt laid prone in his mouth, but when the kid held the joint back up to him, Matt took it.

"Try it again."

With the third hit, a warm vertigo bubbled over the new teenager, and with the fourth try, delicious oblivion. He glanced at the boy, but his eyelids became heavy, and no matter how hard he tried, they wouldn't open any further. All of his teenage angst and frustration drained out through his feet and dissipated into the sand. In fact, for the first time in his life, he felt nothing. His tongue, thick and sluggish in his mouth, struck him as funny, and laughing caused him to only laugh harder. Soon, both boys shook with mirth.

"I'm Evan." The boy's eyes also drooped into slits.

Matthew gasped in a breath and laughed around his own name given back to the teenager.

"You live around here?"

"Yeah, right there." Matt pointed to the house, a little way down the beach. "Do you live here?"

"We just moved in about a week ago."

"Oh, yeah?"

"Ya got anything to eat at your house?" Evan sniffed again.

"Sure," Matthew replied and walked off.

"What about your board?"

"Oh," he giggled, and came back to retrieve it. "You surf?"

"Yeah," Evan replied as they walked to the Taylor house. "Even competed a little."

"Really? Can you do tricks?"

"Oh, hell, yeah," Evan boasted. "I could teach you some."

"That would be so cool."

After they rummaged through the cupboards and came up with some cookies and a jar of pickles, the boys stayed outdoors until evening fell. They talked about surfing, and the kids in the area, while staying high, eating and laughing. Evan stood to leave and gestured at Matt's clothes.

"Make sure you run into the water and scrub your fingers with the sand."

"Why?" Matt asked, looking confused.

"Because if you go in the house like that, your mom will smell it all on your clothes and freak out. Never smoke inside with the windows closed either, or she'll know."

"Oh, okay. Thanks." They made plans for the next day and called out goodbyes as Matthew ran to rinse off in the ocean, then also took a shower as an extra precaution, and started his laundry.

When Dee arrived home, after picking up groceries, she found Matthew sitting on the couch eating potato chips and watching sitcoms.

"Hey, honey," she called out and set the bags on the counter. He grunted, and she walked over to kiss the top of his head. The brim of her hat blocked his view to the screen, and he pushed her away.

"Mom, I'm watchin' Happy Days." Her face fell, and a pang of guilt washed over him.

Several times during the summer, she said she missed him and that the long hours would only be temporary. At first, Matthew vocalized his displeasure, but now he determined it might be an asset. She stepped to the side and watched the TV show for a few moments.

"Hey, you want to get up early and go surfing tomorrow?" she asked.

"No."

"No?" Dee's brow furrowed. "Why not?"

"I met a guy today and we're going all day tomorrow," he said it fast, so he could hear the show's dialogue.

"Oh. Okay, well, who's the guy?"

"His name's Evan."

"Evan, what?"

"I don't know, Mom, just Evan," the teenager barked out, frustrated at being talked to.

"Where did you meet him?"

"At the beach. He just moved here."

"From where?"

"I don't know, okay?" Matthew pushed the button to increase the volume as a man in a red space suit spoke some weird language to young Cunningham, and the laugh track bellowed out their glee.

"Does he know how to surf?" Dee called out over the volume.

At that, her son perked up a little. "Yeah, he's been in competitions even, ever since he was little. He's gonna teach me some tricks."

"Oh," Dee replied, sounding a little disappointed, and retreated into the kitchen. "Maybe after you learn, you could teach me?" she called but received no answer.

At dinner, he only responded to her inquiries in short, irritated responses, before retreating to his bedroom after the meal. He unwrapped the rolled joint, Evan gave him, and after Dee went to bed, opened his bedroom window and lit up. His mother couldn't compete with his new friend, who treated him like an older kid. Numbness saturated his body, and Matt thrilled in the sensation. *Escape.* Tonight, he knew he wouldn't dream.

✳

Dee arrived home and found a strange boy sitting on her couch playing a weird game on the television with Matthew.

"Oh," she said. "Hello, are you Evan?" The boy just grunted and continued to work the joystick with his hands. "What's that?" she asked, observing the television game. "Almost looks like ping pong or tennis." Neither boy said anything, so she glanced at them, then back at the TV. "Isn't that something?"

"It's called Pong, Mom. Evan's parents are rich and his dad works with computers." Matthew's voice broke into the discordant intonation of a boy in the last stages of puberty.

Watching a little longer, Dee stood fascinated as a computerized dot bounced over a dotted line and each boy took turns lobbing it back at the other, in a series of obnoxious bleeps. "Huh, that's cool."

The teenagers continued to ignore her, and she quirked her smile into a frown. "You want to stay for dinner, Evan?" The boy grunted again, and she supposed she'd take that for assent.

"Evan's gonna spend the night tonight too, okay? We're gonna do a marathon."

She agreed with a sigh. The new boy didn't leave their home for two-and-a-half weeks, as the same scenario played out for the rest of the month. The mother grew more tired of the boy and her son's growing disrespect by the day.

"You've got to be kidding me…" Dee scanned the interior of her house several weeks later. Clothes, soda cans, and used dishes with half eaten food dotted the floor and tables, as the television flickered with the same video games she'd seen the boys play all week. Setting down the grocery bags, she opened the refrigerator, the inside stripped of all its contents. "Son of a…" She exhaled her aggression with a growl.

Marching over to the door, she yelled for her son and his friend, but they were nowhere in sight, and by the time they returned for dinner, her blood boiled.

"Hey," she said to them both. "I'm glad you guys are having fun, but I work all day and don't want to come home and spend two hours cleaning up after you, while you sit on your asses." The boys looked at each other, rolled their eyes and grinned. "I mean it!"

"Fine, whatever."

She turned to their squatter. "Evan, you can spend one more night here, but your irritating my wrinkles, and tomorrow you need to go home." He didn't look at her, just grunted. "By the way, I still haven't met your folks. Do you even have folks?" He grunted again, so she asked, "Do they know you're here… again? They gotta be getting worried about you."

"Naw, *they're* cool," he retorted, implying she wasn't. He poignantly scanned her hat and muumuu, then smirked. "And no offense, but you aren't exactly who my parents hang out with. If ya know what I mean."

Matthew giggled cruelly and slapped hands with his friend. Dee looked down at the meal she prepared, pissed off. "Well, I can see that. Most parents around here give a shit where their kids are and make an effort to get to know one another. But you should tell them just because they're trashy and irresponsible doesn't mean they can't still fit in somewhere."

Evan's eyes burned with hurt and anger, but Dee didn't care. She'd had enough of the interloper, his lousy family, and his hold on her son. She glanced at Matt, who glared back at her with livid, piercing eyes. They actually held hatred in them.

She woke that night with a mother's instinct. Closing her eyes, she tried to focus on the sensations she received. A black, snake-like smoke, slow and sinister, wove its way in and around her relationship with Matt, until it burst into flame. Opening her eyes again, her body propelled forward of its own volition. She stood, slid her feet into slippers and wrapped a soft, knitted shawl around her shoulders, before padding out her bedroom door and into the dark hall. Glancing at the clock in the kitchen, it read three in the morning, and she continued her journey to Matt's bedroom. The smell of something foreign wafted into the hall. It took her a moment to identify the pungent aroma of marijuana. However, once marked, she knew it with absolute certainty, after all she did live through the sixties. Worried, she rapped on the door.

"Matthew?" She rustled the doorknob. The two boys, caught in the act, sounded desperate, as they tried to rid themselves of the damning evidence.

The door opened a crack, and Matt's glazed blue eyes stared back at her, "Yeah, Mom?"

His breath reeked of both beer and pot. Dee pushed open the door where Evan still held the joint between thumb and forefinger in front of him, next to an open window. She held out her hand.

"Give it to me."

"What?" the boy asked with obtuse detachment.

"The joint," Dee responded with her voice raised. "Give me the joint."

"Oh," Evan sniggered, eyes half open, and smiled. "Ya wanna hit? Maybe you're cool after all." Matthew barked out a laugh as Evan chuckled at her and his own joke. He extended it out, and she snatched it, before turning a gimlet eye on her son.

"Where did you get the beer?"

The teenager gave her a superior, disinterested shrug, "From the fridge." Dee glared at him, and her jaw clenched. "What's the big deal, Jesus."

"Evan, get your things."

"Why?" the older boy asked.

"'Cause I'm taking you home. Now."

"Like hell you are," Matthew warned, and snatched the joint from his mother's fingers.

She tried to reach for it again, when her son shoved her hard against the wall. Her head cracked against it, denting the sheet-rock. Dazed, she slid down the surface, as a metal wall hanging brought its sharp point against her head, splitting the skin. At first, the two stared at each other and Matt looked worried, then reproachful. He closed the door and locked it, as Evan's explosive laugh muffled behind it, only to have her son join him.

Breathing hard, Dee took a moment to grasp what just happened. Her legs shook and tried to buckle as she stood. Her head throbbed and for the first time in her life, she didn't know what to do. The boys, much taller and stronger, made her feel fearful and alone.

Her boy laughed at her pain. She staggered into the living room, where a telephone beckoned. *Maybe… tough love?* She snatched up the receiver and dialed. Maybe she'd scare the shit out of them. "Kaua'i County Police Department," a confident voice informed her.

Dee held the phone, shaking. *Am I really going to turn my son in for drugs and violence? He'd be in the system, which could lead down a very slippery slope.* Did she really want to do that?

"My mistake," she blurted. "I dialed the wrong number, sorry."

"Are you all right, ma'am?"

She closed her eyes, as they stung with tears and whispered, "Yes, thank you. Sorry." She hung up the phone and slid a hand around to the crown of her throbbing head. Shaking, she drew it back and absorbed the reality of the blood on her fingers.

CHAPTER 9

THE SUNSHINE HIT HER eyes with cruel intentions, and Dee's head seemed to cleave apart. She swung her legs to the side of the bed and reached for her nightstand drawer to relieve it of the bottle of aspirin within. Shaking two round, white tablets onto her palm, she placed them in her mouth and washed them down with the glass of water from her nightstand. Throwing her head back to ensure the medication's successful passage, her gaze floated down and across a red stain on her pillow. Peering closer, she ran her fingers over it and stood on shaking legs. After using the commode, she took up a hand mirror and tried to use it to get visual confirmation of the night before, in the larger wall mirror. A significant dried, brownish-red spot blemished the golden-wheat color of her hair. Two fat tears emerged and trailed down her cheeks before she wiped them away.

Closing eyes to her throbbing temples, Dee placed a quelling hand to the back of her head and stepped gingerly to her closet. She dressed in a colorful yet more subdued muumuu and reached for her hat but thought better of it, and laid it back on the chair. Turning, she stripped the stained pillowcase and sheets before changing and re-making it. The simple chore centered her somewhat before she walked down the hall to her son's door, ready to do battle once more. It stood open and the room empty of occupants.

"Matthew?" she called and received silence in reply. Moving back down the hall toward the kitchen, she called again. "Matt?" As she walked into the kitchen, her gaze swept across her open wallet on the kitchen table.

She growled when she discovered her son and his friend relieved her of all her money. *Damn it, I just got that eighty bucks out yesterday.* Anger bubbled inside her until she screamed out her frustration at the empty room. Taking a deep breath in caused her head to throb, and more tears to well up in her eyes. She grabbed her sunglasses from her purse, then slid them on before going outside. Matthew's bike no longer hung on the wall of the garage, and Evan's no longer lay with reckless abandonment on its side in the yard either.

Livid, Dee drove around for hours and tried to locate them, until weary from emotion and exhaustion, she drove home to a police car parked across her driveway. Panic ricocheted as she tried to listen to her body, but received no warnings. Heart in her throat, she exited the car and walked up to it. Matthew sat handcuffed in the backseat.

"That your son?"

Dee glanced up at the police officer, over six feet in height and a solid ball of muscle. His chin lifted, and nostrils flared as he drew in a deep breath through his nose. His massive muscular chest lifted, and he didn't appear to possess a friendly bone in his body.

"Ah, yes sir," she responded with some hesitation. "I-I've been out looking all over for him."

"He's been drinking out at Grover Stanton's plantation." He peered at the boy, then back at her. "Climbed the water tower and started throwing beer bottles at the livestock."

"Oh my God." Her disgust apparent to all, as she eyed her son through the glass. "What in the hell is wrong with you?"

"Shut up," Matthew slurred. The officer opened the door, and the boy grunted as the man yanked his head back.

"You're digging yourself in deeper there, son. That's no way to talk to your mother." He nodded his head back at Dee. "Stanton said he won't press charges, out of respect for your mother, but if the boy ever comes on his property again, even for a visit, he won't hesitate."

"Yes sir," Dee answered, a little relieved. "I don't think it will happen again… do you, Matthew?"

When the boy said nothing, the officer grabbed the boy by the bicep and hauled him out of the car. "Your mother asked you a question."

"No," he sneered in retort, then stared bleary-eyed at his mother, and grinned. "It won't happen again."

The police officer jerked the boy around and removed his cuffs. Dee scanned the street. Many of their neighbors stood out in their yards, hands up, shielding their eyes from the sun as they watched the spectacle. *Great.* Mortification spread through her as she glanced back at her teenager, who continued to give her the same evil smile.

"If you were my kid, I'd beat your ass," the officer informed him, and Matthew just rolled his eyes, before staggering for the front door. Dejected, Dee followed him.

"Ah, ma'am? Mrs. Taylor?" She turned toward the officer and he laid a broad hand on her shoulder. "Are you okay here?"

"Oh, yes, I'm fine. Thank you."

"You're fine?" He bent to peer into her eyes. "There's an awful lot of blood in your hair. In the back." He gestured toward her hair.

"Oh." Dee reached a hand back to it. "Yes… I tripped and fell over a bunch of crap and hit my head on the wall."

"Uh-huh," he said with suspicion. "Well, if you *fall* again, my name is Marshall Kinney." He withdrew a business card from his pocket, then reached into the patrol car for a pen. He wrote some numbers on the back and handed it to her. "This is my home phone number. I want you to call me, if you have any more… accidents."

Dee tried to smile and took the card. "Thank you, I think he's learned his lesson," she said, but it sounded false even to her own ears.

"Uh-huh," he said again. "Please call me before it gets out of hand. Okay?"

"Okay. Thank you." She gave him a shaky smile, then followed her son's steps into the house.

She closed the door and walked to his room, but the boy laid passed out on his bed, lightly snoring. "Matthew?" Dee prodded him, but he didn't stir.

Deciding she needed some time, she left him there and went out to her garden. For hours, the fragrant dirt and plants moved under her fingers, as she planted fresh life, removed the death, and gained power. *What happened?* They'd been doing so well, surfing all spring and into the summer. Then the business swamped her, and *that boy* came into his life. That's when it started. *How can I stop this? I can't stay with him every second.* She patted the dirt into place, then perceived a presence behind her. Turning, she discovered Matthew watching her.

Dee leaned back to sit on her heels, then stood upright to level the playing field. She stretched her back and faced him. "So, you're up?"

"Yeah."

"What could you possibly have to say for yourself, Matthew?"

"I was just trying to have some fun, for chrissake." He heaved a sigh and rolled his eyes. "There's nothing to do on this stupid island."

"So, you decided to try pot, drink a case of beer, and pushed me into a…"

"You pushed me first."

"What in the hell're talking about, Matty? I never pushed you. I tried to take away the drugs you were smoking."

"Oh, well, I thought you were gonna push me."

"Where in hell did you get the pot from?"

"On the beach. It's easy."

"Oh? And how long have you been engaging in this oh-so-fun activity?"

"Few weeks. It's not that bad, it just chills ya out."

"Yeah, you seem very chill. Evan, get you started on all of that, or have I been missing something all these years?"

"No, well, yeah, I guess technically, but there are a lot of guys on the beach that do it."

"So, you're one of those pathetic followers, then? Thought, what the hell, I'll become a thief, too."

"I'm not a fuckin' thief."

"What do you call stealing beer out of the fridge and taking money from my wallet?"

"You give me money all the time."

"At my choice, Matt! Sometimes I give you money at *my* discretion. When you've earned it, or I know what it's going toward. You knew it was wrong because you did it while I was asleep. Is that where we're at now? Me, locking up my purse at night and having to dictate what you do and who your friends with."

"Oh, fuck that." He glared at her garden, disgusted. "Just dig in your dirt, bitch."

Black rage bubbled throughout her body, and she stepped toward him. "What did you say to me? Just who in the hell do you think you're talking to?"

"I'm sick of you always nagging at me. It's constant! Why can't you just let me be who I am?" he yelled.

"Oh, I'm supposed to let you be a drug addict and a thief," she yelled back. "And let's throw in trespassing, hurting animals, and destruction of property."

"Evan did that."

"I don't give a shit *who* did it. You were there and didn't stop it," she screamed. She sucked air deep into her lungs and let it out through puffed cheeks and pursed lips. "I will *not* have this be my life, Matthew. You're on a very dangerous path and it will lead you nowhere, except a burnout on the beach or dead."

"Better than a middle-aged hag, who dresses stupid and thinks everything's perfect all the time." He sneered at her. "Do you even know what the kids say about you? You're a fucking joke, with your stupid hat and ugly-ass clothes? You think you're some kind of mother." He laughed. "You gave shit to Evan about his parents, when you do the exact same thing, ya hypocrite. It's embarrassing."

"You don't know the first thing about embarrassment. Mortification is your son coming home in a police car with the entire neighborhood out working in their yards. And as for the rest of it, I don't give a shit! So, the joke's on them, son, because I'm happy with who I am. I *know* who I am. I'm sorry I can't be here with you every day, all day. Don't you think I would if I could? Surfin', watching TV, and having fun? *Someone* has to earn the living and buy all the shit you destroy and leave hanging around. Your father…" She tried to tell him about how Arthur gave her the hat because he understood her but couldn't finish the words.

"Is fucking dead. Dad's dead, Grandma's dead. Move on, Dee, everyone else has." And with that her son returned to the house and slammed the door with a loud reverberating bang.

Dee closed her eyes to the pain of it, as if he'd punch her hard in the stomach. Looking out to the ocean, she listened to the peaceful waves churning onto the shore and yearned for her husband's and mother's presence and guidance. For the rest of the afternoon, Dee worked, trying to map out how to proceed. By the time she called him back out, she was ready and drew her line in the sand.

"You aren't going to see Evan again. Stop…" She held up a hand when he tried to speak. "It's non-negotiable. He is no longer welcome in this house. You will come back to work at the shop with me, and you're grounded for the rest of the summer."

"Like hell I am," he spat. "You aren't the one in charge anymore, Dee."

"Yes. I am." She withdrew Officer Kinney's business card from the pocket of her muumuu and showed it to him. "It's that officer's card. He saw the blood on the back of my head, and now you're on his radar." She placed it back into her pocket and studied her son. "He said all I have to do is call him. Now, I don't want to do that because it will put you on a path that could ruin your entire life, but the way you're behaving, Matthew, you've already taken steps down that path. I'm not gonna just watch it happen. I love you too much."

Matthew stared down at his shoes.

"You want to live a life in and out of jail? People making judgements about you in twenty years because of stupid choices you're making right now? You can hate me all you want, but I won't stand by and do nothing."

"Evan says…"

"Evan's a piece of shit. He's angry and bitter. A malicious boy, whose parents don't give a shit about him, and he wants you to share in his misery so he doesn't feel so alone. I can't help him. He's not my son, thank God, and he's not your friend. And he sure as hell is no longer in your life." She waited until Matthew looked her in her eyes. "If he steps one foot onto my property again, I'll have him arrested for trespassing. If I, or anyone I know, see you in his company, I will bust him for drugs and anything else I can think of. Do you understand me?" When Matt didn't speak, she barked, "Do you understand me, son?"

He flinched and nodded. "Now, go inside and clean up your room and yourself, then we'll make dinner together." He retreated into the house and Dee let out a breath she didn't realize she'd been holding.

She knelt on the grass, at the foot of the banyan tree, and sat, legs bent back on either side of her. "I need help," she whispered. "I can't lose him too. Arthur? Mama?" she pleaded. "Can you hear me? Send me some help." The wind rustled through the tree, but peace did not come.

CHAPTER 10

JUNE 1979

D EE PUSHED A SEED into a small cup and gently folded dirt over the top of it, before setting it aside. She reached for another one when a shadow fell over her.

"Hello, Mrs. Taylor." She turned and met the eyes of Officer Marshall Kinney. His warm chocolate eyes and mouth crinkled into a smile. "How have you been?"

"Oh, I'm good." She brushed dirty hands off on her work apron. "We're both good. How are you?"

"Well, I've driven past here a million times, but never stopped in."

"Well, I'm glad you did today? Is there something I can help you find?" She took in his Rolling Stones tee-shirt, well-worn jeans and tennis shoes. He sure didn't look like a police officer now. No longer threatening or unkind.

"No, it actually… Well, to be honest, I was working myself up to seeing if you wanted to have dinner with me sometime."

"Oh." Surprised, Dee blushed, then grinned. "Wow, okay, well, I haven't done this in a while. Um, I didn't even know you were interested."

"I'm interested." He smiled and his own cheeks reddened a bit. "What do you think? It can be coffee, if you'd rather not have dinner… or maybe a drink?"

"Ah, well…" Her mind raced over the possibilities. "Sure, that would be really nice."

"Great! How about tonight?"

"All right, what time?"

"Well, how 'bout I pick you up at your house at about 6:30?"

"6:30. Okay, that sounds great. Thank you, ah…" She blushed again, unsure how to address him.

"Just go with Marshall," he said, reading her thoughts, "and I'll go with Dee."

Giggling, she nodded. "Okay, Marshall it is."

"Kay, well, I'll see ya tonight then."

"See ya tonight." She watched him walk away, then caught Evie's eye. Her best friend grinned at her like a Cheshire cat. "Oh, shut up," Dee called, but the grin grew even bigger.

Matthew opened the door and flinched at the familiar, giant policeman standing in his doorway. Except for the fact that the man wasn't dressed like an officer. Matt's eyes narrowed as Kinney smiled at him.

"Good evening, Matthew." Marshall gave a lift of his head in greeting.

"What do you want?"

"I'm here to pick up your mother. How have you been? Stayin' out of trouble?"

Matthew just blinked at him. His mother said she was going out with a friend that night but made no mention it was a date. Now, what, she was dating the fucking cop! Pissed, Matt turned into the house and called, "Dee, your *date's* here."

Nervous and twitchy his mother came around the corner, in a periwinkle dress with bright pink hibiscus flowers on it, and her hair coiled inside her hat with several hues of plumeria flowers encircling the brim. Matt scowled even more. When she noticed Kinney still stood on the porch she hissed, "Why didn't you ask him in?"

"Cause I didn't want him to come in." He walked back to his bedroom and slammed the door.

He heard them exchange muffled words, then Dee called out a goodbye and said she'd be home before ten and they left. Frustrated, Matt grabbed his duck-taped

wallet fifteen minutes later and left through the back
door to walk down the beach a way. He spotted Evan
in the middle of *his* group of friends. They were all
moving on without him.

"Hey," Evan sneered. "There's the mama's boy.
What're you doing off your leash, man?"

"Come here," Matt called, and giving him a cold
look, Evan walked over and lit a cigarette.

"What?" The boy blew out a thick stream of smoke.
"Better not get seen with me, or your mommy will
have a heart attack."

"Fuck off. What in the hell am I supposed to do?
Do you have a couple already rolled?"

"Maybe."

"Do you or don't you?"

"Two."

"How much."

Evan grinned. "What about your mom?"

"She went out with the fuckin' cop."

Evan's eyes widened at that. "Well, what the hell're
you doing here, man? Stay the fuck away from me."
He retreated a step back.

"Come on, just sell me a couple smokes. I already
told you were still gonna hang out, I just gotta be
careful."

"Fuck you."

"Evan. Come on. Please?"

An evil grin slithered across Evan's face. "All right, I'll tell you what. You split up your bitch and the cop and I'll keep you high and happy. Even give ya a little blow."

"What's blow?"

"Cocaine, you idiot… Jesus." Evan pulled out two joints and a small baggie containing some white powder, but held it out of Matt's grasp. "But I won't sell you shit, if your mom dates the cop. Bust it up."

"Okay, I promise."

Dee had a fantastic night. All the early nervousness vanished in the first five minutes of the car ride. He wasn't Arthur, but he wasn't supposed to be. By the time they ate dinner, had a cocktail and he drove her back to her house, she had a beautiful warm glow heating her from within. Marshall walked around the car, opened the door for her, then extended a hand to help her out.

Standing close together, the streetlight illuminated them, and he stroked a hand down Dee's cheek. "You are a very beautiful woman, Dee."

"Hmm, I like you. Maybe I'll keep you around for a while." She giggled. "And blind."

"I'd like that."

"What! You're into bondage?"

He grinned and without another word he leaned down and laid his lips on her own. The deep tugs of longing pulled within her, and she opened his mouth with hers, allowing her tongue to explore him. Both hummed, and she opened her eyes to find him watching her. Cupping the back of her head with one hand, he allowed the other to glide down the side of her neck. *God, yes!*

When they parted, Marshall smiled down at her. "It was a great night. Thanks for coming out with me?."

"Well, thanks for asking. You are a fantastic kisser."

His laugh echoed off the nearby homes and quiet night. "Right back at you. Call you tomorrow?"

"Okay." She whispered, then reached behind her for the doorknob. "Thanks again, good night."

"Night." He gave a wave and another grin before walking back to his car.

She walked inside and closing her eyes, leaned back against the door with a sigh. When she opened them again, Matthew sat on the sofa staring at her, furious.

"Matty, what are you doing?"

"Waiting for you."

"Oh." She went to the hallway table and set down her purse and keys. "Did you find the food I made for you?"

"Yeah."

She turned to consider him. He'd been crying. "Matty? What's wrong?"

"Why did you go out with him?"

"Marshall?" Her brow furrowed. "I…"

"You didn't even ask if I was okay with it."

"Ah… Well… Are you okay with it."

"No! Are you kidding!"

"He's a really nice man, Matt. You'd like him, if you got to know him."

"I don't want to get to know him. Why do you like hurting me?"

"What?"

"Don't you think I'm already enough of a freak?"

"Matt, what in the hell are you talking about? Of course you're not a freak."

He stood up, glaring at her. "Yes, I am. I'm the kid whose dad got chopped up in a harvester. I'm the one whose grandma died in the grocery store," he screamed and started to cry again. "I'm the one whose mom talks to trees and wears stupid clothes and is all weird all the time. I'm the one who had to read that letter in front of the whole school!"

"Matt…"

"I'm the one whose mom is now going to start fucking a cop…"

"Hey!"

"No one will ever want to come over here and hang out. No one will ever want me to go to parties because a cop could show up." His voice became choked with genuine frustration. "You always said if you had any extra time you wanted to hang out with me, but it's all a lie! And now all you're gonna want to do is hang out with him. And he's going to be here all the time and want me to change and do things his way. Pretty soon it will you and him, and not me and you, and I'll be alone."

"Matt, honey." She ran over to him and hugged him to her. "Shh."

"Why can't it ever just be me? You and me? Why aren't I ever good enough?"

"You are good enough, Matt. It's always going to be you and me first. Before anyone else. Look, I don't need to start this. If you aren't ready, that's fine, honey. We'll figure it all out." She stroked his hair. "I promise you, that you are the most important person in my life, Matt, always."

She sighed and held him close, stroking his hair. Tomorrow she would call Marshall and explain she wasn't ready.

CHAPTER 11

SEPTEMBER 1981

MATTHEW WALKED ALONG THE Makawehi Cliffs near Shipwreck beach in the middle of the night. He and his mother settled into a truce over the past three years. They started surfing together again, and she tried to keep a regular schedule, but things never got easy between them. He'd meant everything he said to her that night, but also thought she probably resented him for not allowing her a personal life of her own. *She doesn't need a personal life. She has me. I'm enough.*

There was no way in hell Matt would ever let go of something that allowed him to escape from his anger and the nightmares of drowning and demons he'd experienced most of his life. When he realized the geographic location of his bedroom provided him an easy escape route, he frequently forayed into the darkness of the wee hours of morning to meet with friends, drink, experiment with drugs, risky behavior and sex. Given how hard Dee worked, he knew his mother, once asleep, never woke until morning.

He'd also let his mother believe the friendship between Evan and himself dissolved, but they often hung out together during the night's escapades.

Yet tonight, he walked the mile and a half from his house to Shipwreck beach searching for solitude. To sit alone on the cliffs and smoke with his own thoughts. Upon arrival, he discovered a pretty girl sitting in his favorite spot, smoking her own cigarette.

"Hey, what's up?"

Her cynical eyes lifted and scanned him as she took another drag off her cigarette. "Not much. Who are you?"

"Matt." He sat down next to her and withdrew papers and a small baggie of bud from his shirt pocket. He rolled it into a joint but looked up on occasion to meet her amused gaze.

"You've got cool eyes," she observed, then eyed the blunt between his forefinger and thumb with longing.

He gave a lopsided grin and raised it. "Wanna hit?"

"Sure." She shrugged and took it from him.

"What's your name?"

"Drea," she said on an exhale and handed the drug back to him.

"Drea?"

"Yeah." She kicked her legs back and forth, as they dangled over the edge of the jagged cliff, and he followed suit.

"So, what's your story?" he asked, smoking, then handed the joint back to her as she shrugged again.

"Came down here with a group." She dragged long and deep off the joint, and her small chest lifted and thrust out as she closed her eyes.

"How long you staying?"

"Til the universe tells me it's time to go," she replied with implied wisdom and lifted her face to the pearly moon. She opened her eyes to find him scanning her body.

"That's cool." He lifted his eyes to hers, on an exhale of breath, and reclaimed the joint. "How old are you?"

"Just turned fifteen."

"I turned fifteen in June."

"Cool."

"You run away?"

"Yeah."

"Where from?"

"Oregon."

He thought she lied about the place, but said, "That's cool. Your parent's assholes?"

"My dad is. My mom's like this total bitch. You?"

"My dad's dead. Dee, my mom… she's a total pain in my ass." Feeling a little guilty because in fact, they were doing pretty well together at the moment. He covered his discomfort with a cough.

Drea nodded in agreement. "Aren't they all?"

They talked for a few hours, and after a while, she peered down on the beach below their feet, hair lifting in the wind, and wafting a floral scent to his nostrils.

"Ya wanna walk down there?" he asked.

"What's down there?"

"Some caves and the beach." He raised his brows at her. *We could hook up.*

Drea seemed to understand his implication, and they climbed down to walk along the sand holding hands. After a few minutes, he stopped and drew her to him. His hands framed her face, then moved down her neck and shoulders as he kissed her. Taking one of his hands in her own, she placed it on her breast and pulled him down onto the beach with her other. Matthew sat down and she straddled his hips, kissing him with eagerness.

"Ya got anything harder on the island than that?" she asked and nodded at the small stub of pot and paper.

"You mean besides my dick?"

"Oh my God." Touching the object in question, they both dissolved into uncontrollable giggles. "Tell ya what," she panted. "If you find me an actual party… I can take care of *that* right now."

"What kind of party you want?"

"Ever done Smack?"

Two days later, Dee stood at the stove making some fried chicken, when the front door opened, announcing her son's arrival. She winced as the screen door slammed behind him with a loud report.

"Matthew, what did I tell you about slamming the door?" The stink of cigarette smoke arrived before her son did. Sighing, Dee wiped her hands on a towel in resignation. *It would be one of those nights.* She walked around the corner, and almost into a disheveled, thin-wisp of a girl hanging on her son's arm. "Oh," Dee said, startled. "Ah… hi?" When the girl said nothing, Dee glanced at her offspring.

"Dee, Drea." He nodded his head toward the girl. "Drea, Dee." He nodded his head the other way toward his mother. "She's my new girl."

Dee's eyes widened at the proclamation, then returned to the girl, a mere inch shorter than her son's 5'11" frame. Her long strawberry blonde hair, styled in a typical Farrah Fawcett do, feathered back from a face still rounded with youth. Red-rimmed hazel eyes featured too much peacock-blue eyeshadow and black eyeliner, while her hollow cheeks contained red circles of blush. Dee guessed the girl to be about fifteen or sixteen.

At a loss, she extended her hand. "Ah, nice to meet you–Drea- was it?"

"Yeah. Damn, something smells good." She moved past her and into the kitchen, then peered into the frypan.

Dee darted her eyes to her son and drew her brows together in question, but he just grinned back at her.

"Isn't she cool?" he murmured, "I asked her to stay for dinner. Is that okay?"

"I see that. How old is she?"

"Like seventeen."

"My ass…"

"Can she stay for dinner or not?" he asked, exasperated.

"Ah." He viewed the girl like a new puppy, and two things struck her. One, he wanted to impress the girl and two, he tried to be courteous in the original asking. Looking for an opportunity to have another connection with her son, even if a small and tenuous one, she relented. "I guess. It's just fried chicken, green beans and salad."

"That'll work."

"So, Drea," Dee asked when they sat down at the table. "Where are you from?"

The girl ignored her and reached across Matt for the green beans. As she scooped out the vegetables onto her plate, she blew a bubble with her bubble gum. Dee drew her brows together and peered at her son, who smiled whether smitten or at the girl's lack of manners, she didn't know.

"So, where did you guys meet?" Dee tried again.

"On the cliffs," Matt responded.

"Makawehi?"

"Yeah."

"When?" Dee watched the girl take about three sticks of masticated gum out of her mouth and lay it on her table. Dumfounded, she now narrowed her eyes at the girl in disapproval. "Ah, Drea?"

"What?"

"Could you please take your gum off the table? This was my mother's."

Drea gave an inpatient grunt and lifted defiant eyes to Dee. The older woman stared back at her, taking on the challenge and sharpening her eyes.

"Here just put it on your plate," Matt suggested, not realizing he saved both women from losing face or drawing blood.

For the rest of the meal, Drea spoke few words and inhaled her dinner. The couple left the table without acknowledgement or thanks for the home-cooked meal, and unease wafted over Dee. When Matthew returned from bringing the girl back to the group she lived with, his mother waited for him with a cup of tea, a soft blanket across her lap and an enjoyable book.

"Hey." He inclined his head toward her as he walked through the door.

"Hey." She smiled, glancing up from her book. "So, did you get her home okay?"

"Yeah." He took off his sweatshirt and threw it on the couch before sitting down.

Delighted with the company, she closed her book and set it on the end table, before taking up her tea for a sip.

"She's a beautiful girl, Matty."

"Yeah," he grinned. "She's cool."

Easy, Dee, think about the best way to approach this. "She about your age then?" she asked, trying for an air of ambivalence.

"Yeah, fifteen," he admitted.

"Mm hmm, nice," Dee replied and pulled off her blanket. She stood and walked toward the kitchen and called over her shoulder, "She move on island with her family or just visiting?" She busied herself making another cup of tea for her son with the remaining water.

"No, she's here with a bunch of friends."

Dee peered out over the darkened dining room as she dipped the tea bag in and out of the water. *So, she is a runaway.* Sighing, she lifted the mug and carried it back into the living room illuminated by her single table lamp. She tried to hand the cup to Matt, whose eyes were closed and head bobbed.

"Here ya go, Matty."

His eyes opened and took the mug, sniffing the fruit and floral contents of the liquid, before sipping it. "Oh, thanks."

"How long she staying for?"

"Til the universe tells her it's time to go home… or something like that."

"Ah." Dee nodded at the implied wisdom. "Drea… it's a cool name." She eyed her son over the rim of her own mug. "What's her last name?"

"I don't know."

"Hmm. What part of the mainland is she from?"

"I can't remember where she said. Why?"

"No reason," Dee responded, cautious now. "She just talked little at dinner, and I'm curious to get to know her better."

The teenager drew his brows together, then turned his head on an eye roll, and set his mug of tea on the coffee table. *And I lost him, again.* He stood and walked toward his bedroom.

"Night, Matty," she called out.

"Night."

In a lower voice, she quipped with irritation, "Why, you're so welcome for dinner, son." Standing, she picked up the mugs. "Nice chit-chatting with you as we pretend not to know your new girlfriend ran away from home and must have parents worried sick about her." She poured the tea out and placed the cups into the dishwasher. "What about, 'hey Mom, I wanna bring a friend over for dinner,'" she said mimicking her son, then switched back to herself. "Oh, no problem, thanks for askin'." She turned the machine on and wiped down the counter, throwing the washcloth into the sink with more force than she intended. Leaning back onto the counter, she blew out a formidable breath.

Her gaze shifted to the family photo of her, Arthur, and Matt on the wall. They stood out in the surf, a wave crashing around them for their first photo together. Arthur laughed, beaming out positivity and hope, while Dee gazed down at her newborn, holding his chubby bare foot. A new family full of promise and possibility. Now, the broken reality, Arthur dead fourteen years. Mama, gone eleven. A girl at her table, glaring at her for having the audacity to speak. *Maybe I'll get lucky and she'll get bored and just disappear.* Pursing her lips, she knew better and turned the light out on the photo of the contented trio.

CHAPTER 12

DEE LOOKED FORWARD TO her yearly girls' weekend getaway with Evie. This trip made even more special as Evie and Issac were moving to the mainland in a few months. Though they still vowed to see each other, Dee knew the tradition less likely to continue, as time moved on, and the thought radiated sadness to her core.

"I think we just have enough time for coffee and a bear claw," Evie said. "The exhibit opens at ten, right?"

"Yes," Dee replied, straightening her hat. She used seed packages and compost pods as her circlet today, with a ridiculous monkey on a wire bobbing in front of her, to everyone's delight. "I'll get a map on how to get there from the front desk. Wanna just meet at the coffee stand?"

"Oakally, Dokeally."

Dee hummed to herself as she waited for the woman at the front desk to finish a call.

"Hey Dee," The clerk pushed a button and placed the receiver on its cradle. "Great timing. You have a phone call."

"Really?"

"Yeah, do you want me to send it to your room or…"

"Oh, no." She walked up to the podium. "I'll take it here. Can I also get a map for downtown?"

"Sure." She handed her the phone and released more of the phone cord, before looking for the stack of hotel maps.

"Hello, this is Dee Taylor. Who's this?"

"Hi, Dee, it's Marcy Henderson, down the street."

Dee smiled, thinking of the woman she'd asked to water her flowers and monitor Matthew while she traveled for the weekend.

"Hey there, everything okay?"

"Well… No, not really." Dee took a deep breath and listened, her face growing redder with each word uttered.

Furious, she hung up the phone and straightened her hat. She could see the plastic monkey attached on the wire bounce with frivolity in her periphery and crossed her arms. Resigned and disappointed at the loss of her one weekend to relax and hang out with her best friend, she met Evie and explained the situation. After checking out, she boarded a puddle jumper back to Kaua'i.

She turned the corner to her home two hours later. Cars remained parked in her driveway, on her grass and down the street. Individuals flicked cigarette butts into her prize hibiscus plants and walked in and out of her house as if they lived there. The music, cranked up to an obscene decibel, pulsated out of the dwelling, packed with teenagers and young adults. Mouth dropped open, Dee scanned her house and what used to pass as a quiet neighborhood. She paid the driver, stepped out of the cab with her suitcase and walked inside. Kids of all ages sat, stood and swayed with the same vacant expressions wafting across their faces. Some did a double take with their eyes as she passed by them, appearing to recognize her.

Colorful liquid pooled in the carpet, as hundreds of cups turned over on tables and chairs, leaking their contents all over. The smell of cigarettes and pot lingered everywhere. Greasy pizza containers sat on her mother's table and when she lifted them, permanent heat stains left burns, along with a lot of white powder on its surface. The room tilted as her eyes fell on her son leaning against a counter in the kitchen. Drea sat on the countertop behind him, arms and legs wrapped around his shoulders and mid-section, holding some kind of pipe up to his lips. He inhaled whatever waterlogged drug was in the pipe and blew out steamed smoke.

Dee maneuvered over to her sound system, face scarlet, and hit the power button. The room fell silent, and she screamed, "Get the fuck… out… of *my* house!" Everyone stared at her in stupidity. "Get out, or I swear by Christ, every single one of you pathetic pieces of shit will go to jail." Some kids retorted in curses, but when she crossed the room, picked up the house phone, and pretended to dial, they moved.

"Officer Kinney," she spoke in a raised voice, to a dial tone. "This is Dee Taylor at 510 Hoona Road. I came home to find my son, Matthew, having a party with an enormous group of other minors. There're drugs and…" The kids, many knowing the officer's name, moved in greater haste toward the doors. "Yes sir, I'll start taking names until you get here."

She hung up and grabbed for a pad of paper, but seeing her camera, grabbed it instead and started to take pictures of the kids. The frenzy that now moved through doors and even some windows impressed even her. As Matthew approached her, high and sluggish, he reached out to take the camera from her.

"What the fuck, Mom?"

She slapped him hard across the face, and he stumbled into the table. Reaching a hand up to his cheek, he stared at his mother in disbelief, who stood shaking with rage.

"Jesus, chill out, Dee," Drea bitched.

Something inside her snapped, and she turned her wrath onto the girl who had some residual intelligence to shut up.

"Get the fuck out of my house, Drea," she ordered, then turned her ire toward her son. "You will clean up every bit of this or you will spend as long as they'll have you in jail, and I will not bail you out." Her eyes returned to square off with Drea, who blanched, and turned on her heel, cursing. Dee followed and slammed the front door in the girl's face, when she turned to spit more vile obscenities, and locked it. Taking a deep breath, Dee laid a hand on the closed door, then grabbed her carry-on suitcase and retreated to her room without another word to her son.

When Dee woke the next morning, she took inventory. Matthew had attempted to pick up the house. Though nowhere near considered clean, the trash and bottles now lived in large black plastic bags rather than the furniture. He'd wiped the countertops, but a sticky film remained on them. Her mother's tabletop still contained burn marks, as did various cabinets, where guests extinguished their cigarettes on them or allowed them to burn unchecked on their surface. Her slippers stuck to the floor as she walked, and when she opened the back-slider door, she discovered parts of her gardens trampled. Opening the door wider, she let the warm wind blow over her as she took in her destroyed sanctuary. Not able to see it the night before in the dark, Matthew missed most of the trash outside, and all the clothes from kids skinny dipping in the ocean. At least she hoped that's what occurred, the alternative being sex in her backyard under the watchful gaze of Marcy Henderson. He stood by the banyan tree, looking out toward the ocean.

"You missed a lot," Dee said without sympathy. "Finish it now, and then I want you out of my house."

She turned without saying another word and walked back toward the kitchen. She made herself a cup of coffee to steady her nerves, as Matthew followed her through the slider. He sat down at the kitchen table and noticed the burn marks on the table as if for the first time. He ran a hand over them, then glanced up at his mother.

"Sorry, Mom," he mumbled, looking down at the table again.

"I'm not interested and don't want to hear anything else from you anymore. I'm just done." Stone-faced, Dee walked to the table and sat down with her coffee. When she said nothing else, Matt struggled to look her in the face. He leaned back in his chair and closed his eyes. She still didn't respond when he opened his eyes again, so he divulged, "She's pregnant, Mom."

Of all the things her son could've said somehow, *she's pregnant*, loomed furthest from her imagination. Although, in hindsight, she guessed it shouldn't be that big of a shock. Her mouth dropped open as the breath punched from her lungs.

"Pregnant?" When he just nodded in confirmation, she goggled at him. "Since when?"

"I guess a while. She took a test."

"A doctor's test or just like a drug store test?"

"A drug store test, but she did a few of 'em."

"So, what… you thought, let's throw a party? To what? Celebrate?"

"No, I think I just like freaked out," he replied, not looking at her. "I don't know what to do. She says she wants to keep it, and I don't get to say anything about it."

Dee could see the terror and desperation in his eyes now. Her heart pounded, and mind raced, trying to reason it out and searched for the right things to say. *If she wasn't pregnant, they'd need to find that out, and if she was, well, they'd have to cross that bridge when they came to it.*

"Okay." Dee drew in a breath and let it out through her nose. "Well, she needs to go to the doctor, to make sure."

"You think she's lying?"

"I don't know if she's lying, Matthew. You guys are fifteen years old!" she ended with a bellow. "If she is, you need to know about it and if she isn't, then there're things we need to do. Get a doctor for one, if she's keeping it. Vitamins, for another, for a healthy baby. Maybe stop drinking and smoking things that come in glass pipes, so your baby has an actual chance."

Dee stood and walked to the phone to call their primary physician and secured an appointment at the clinic for that afternoon.

"Okay," she said, returning to the table. "She's got an appointment at four o'clock. You need to go with her and be in the room when they give her the results."

"What do I do until four?"

"You clean up my fucking house," she replied with disgust. "They trashed my gardens. The floor needs mopping, the carpets need vacuuming, and shampoo-ing. The cabinets need to be wiped down." His eyes filled with resignation.

"Okay." Tears splashed onto the table and his shoul-ders slumped. "I'm sorry about Kupuna's table, and the house, and everything. I don't know why I did it."

"You don't know why because there's no good reason for it. You are out of control," she said with frost, and he cried louder. "You've broken trust with me so many times, Matt, I can't even count them anymore. And if that girl's pregnant, your entire life's about to change. I'll help you as best as I can, but…" She reached out a hand to his. "The time for being a selfish kid is now over. You made the grown-up choice to have unprotected sex with her, and now your options are more limited. If she's pregnant, you gotta do right by that child. Nothing else matters now."

"I know," he murmured. "But I don't know what to do, Mom." His eyes pleaded with hers. "Will you help me?"

"I will. But I also won't tolerate any more upheaval in my life, Matt. Zero." She lifted his chin and looked him in the eye. "I don't deserve it, Matthew. Do you understand me?" He nodded.

She spent the day laboring to repair her gardens and work off her mad. When the couple arrived back home, they informed her Drea's pregnancy counted six weeks in duration. Dee asked for proof, and he thrust out a piece of paper toward his mother. She accepted it to read the confirmation. As Matthew spoke, Dee's gaze shifted to the girl who stared back at her in smug satisfaction. The look intensified when Matthew asked his mother if she could move in with them. *If I tell them to leave, and they continue their lifestyle, this baby won't stand a chance. If they stay, maybe a miracle can happen, and they'll grow up with the impending responsibility.*

"Drea can move in here *until* you get the money together for an apartment, but there *will* be rules." Dee looked directly at the girl, then her son. "No drugs of any kind, in any form, is tolerated inside my house or in my gardens, and that includes cigarettes.

This is non-negotiable. I will expect both of you to keep the common areas clean and to pick up after yourselves. You'll ask my permission before anyone… I don't care if it's one person or five people, comes into *my* home again." Her eyes sharpened on Drea. "And you *will* see a doctor every month, and follow his or her instructions, to create a healthy, content baby or I'll have you charged with endangerment, and any other legal thing I can throw at you. If you can both agree to that, you can stay here for a short time."

She hadn't finished speaking before Matthew started to nod his head in agreement. Dee eyed the girl who gave a snide shrug of her shoulders. It would have to be enough.

"Hey," Drea grunted a few weeks later, holding a bowl that overflowed with milk and cereal.

Dee's head popped up from scrubbing the floor on her hands and knees. "Good morning. I see you're up bright and early." Dee glanced up at the clock on the wall that read 11:45 AM. "Ready to get out there and look for a job today, Drea?"

"No, I was hungry."

"Ah," Dee replied, and returned to her cleaning. She needed to get back to the shop for inventory but didn't want the domestic chore to go another day uncompleted.

"So, did Matt tell you I might not want to be pregnant anymore?"

Dee stopped scrubbing again and looked at the girl who grinned at the older woman's discomfort. "You what?"

"Yep." The girl took a huge bite of cereal and spoke around the mouthful. "The doctor says I need to decide soon."

Dee stood, breathing a little harder, and searched the floor for inspiration. "You're nine weeks already, Drea."

"I know that, Dee," she mimicked. "I'm not stupid, ya know."

Dee gave the girl a look that implied the pronouncement debatable, then tried to soften. "Okay. Well, I guess we should talk about…"

"No. It's not *your* decision, it's *my* decision," she whined like a petulant child. The older woman remained silent as the girl continued her diatribe. Whatever she said next, Drea would do the opposite.

"Right," Dee agreed. "No, you're right. You guys are way too young to take care of a baby. It would never work."

Surprised, Drea stared at her. No doubt she hoped Dee would express the desire to become a grandmother. "You *want* me to get rid of it?"

"Well, dear, it's clear you aren't mother material, now are you? When you're not pregnant, you drink and do drugs. an absolute junkie."

"I'm not a junkie."

"You aren't very nurturing," Dee continued as if she hadn't spoken. "You don't know how to cook. Hell, you can't even keep a bathtub clean." She gestured to the bucket of sudsy water. "And Matthew, he'd be a terrible father." Dee gave a smug look back at the girl. "If you got rid of it now, you could go back to your self-absorbed lifestyle. Even though you said you wouldn't, there's no way in hell you could make it another thirty-one weeks without a small toke here and there just because you're pregnant. You're incapable of staying clean, and everyone knows it."

"How would you know anything?"

"Because you have no self-control and you're a selfish, entitled brat, dear," Dee replied with sugar, hoping her gamble paid off. "Having a healthy pregnancy and a grown-up life isn't something you're built for because you're a little girl who doesn't give a shit about anyone but herself."

"I could do it if I wanted to," Drea spat, her eyes black with hatred. "I just don't want to."

Dee's heartbeat sped up, but responded, "Exactly. No shame in saying you *can't* do it." She removed her gloves and set them on the counter and grabbed the girl's wrist, propelling her toward the telephone. "Here, let's go call the clinic and get you scheduled for an abortion right away. You'll feel so much better. It'll hurt like hell, but you'll be well rid of it."

Drea jerked her hand out of Dee's and threw her full bowl of cereal at her, before running back into the bedroom she shared with Dee's son. She screeched at her teen lover, telling him his mother wanted to murder their baby, but she wouldn't allow it. Dee could hear Matthew speak, groggy from sleep.

"I thought you said you didn't want it, anyway."

"I never said that," Drea screamed back.

"Yes, you did. You said…"

"And that crazy bitch isn't gonna tell me who I am, or what I can do with my own body. Do you know what she said to me?"

Dee removed her hat still dripping with milk and peeked around the corner. Her son sat half erect in the bed, hair looking like a raccoon slept in it all night, observing his baby mama with red and bleary eyes.

"She said I wouldn't be a good mom, or be able to take care of the baby," Drea's eyes swam with false tears. "We need to get out of this house, Matty. I wanna go, right now. Right now!"

Matthew observed his mother in the doorway and her eyebrows raised in question. They'd been working as a team again in the weeks since the big announcement. His eyes held genuine sorrow in them, whether for her or his cushy life evaporating, she didn't know. He wrapped an arm around his girlfriend's thin shoulders.

"Okay, fine, we'll move out, but freaking out isn't good for the baby or you."

"Oh, and how are you going to do that?" Dee asked and walked into full view, replacing her hat on her head.

"I'll quit school… I wasn't gonna pass this year, anyway."

"Matty," Dee said, surprised. "You can't do that. It's only one more year. Your choices go down to nothing if you don't have a high school degree."

"You don't have one."

"But I… I…" She wanted to say she had to help put food on the table, but now, he needed to do the same thing. She searched his filthy room for inspiration but came up with nothing.

"Can I come work for you?" he shrugged.

"I can't pay you enough to support an entire family, Matt." Dee experienced genuine panic, at a loss for how to help him.

"I've got to do this, Ma." Matt sighed and placed a hand on her shoulder. "We should've done it a long time ago." Drea smirked and walked past Dee, throwing a shoulder into hers. Mother and son looked at each other for a long moment. "I'm sorry. We were turning it around, weren't we?" She nodded, and her eyes flooded with tears. The past three weeks they worked together better than they ever had before. "It'll be the best thing all around. You'll get some peace.

I'll get some peace." He lifted an eyebrow, and they grinned at each other. He stood in boxers and drew on some sweats from a clothes heap on the floor. Locating a sweatshirt, he smelled it, and wrinkled his nose, but thread arms through the sleeves, before walking over and wrapping arms around her. The sweatshirt had a sour odor to it, as if left in the washer for days before being placed in the dryer. He hugged her until Drea resumed her screeching at him from the front yard.

Inspired, Dee said, "Hey, I'll try to give Bert Norton's son a call." She patted his back. "He's running the plantation now. It's not sugar anymore, it's coffee, but you can learn. I know he'll take you on and if you dig in, it could give you a real good life, Matt. But I gotta tell you upfront, if you drink or do drugs or screw up, he'll get rid of you and then you really *will* be lost."

"Okay." He nodded and grabbed his wallet. "I won't fuck it up. Thanks, Mom." He squeezed her hand before walking out to his new uncertain life.

Dee never told Matt about the money accruing interest over the years, or what she set aside for him. It was the most logical choice. She didn't think Matthew stupid enough to leave the island because he understood they needed help. Drea remained the unknown entity. The couple found affordable housing near the Lihue airport and moved in. Sugar Grove Plantation, now known as Grove Industries, hired Matthew but living on a small island his reputation for drugs preceded him, and the employer set a condition of random and mandatory drug screenings. For the first time in his life, the younger Taylor assumed responsibility for himself and future family by showing up to work on time and getting clean through Alcoholics and Narcotics Anonymous.

On the gorgeous, perfect morning of July 15th, 1982, Finn Matthew, entered the Taylor's world. A long baby at twenty-three inches, the infant weighed a healthy eight pounds, two ounces. *The girl did it*, and Dee closed her eyes with relief. Drea never touched a drop of alcohol or ingested any drugs for the remainder of her pregnancy. It would be the one and only thing Finn's mother would do for him, unless you counted leaving, which she did two weeks later.

Dee plucked a new mango hanging low on the tree in the Cornucopia gardens and examined it. *Perfection*. A shadow fell over her and she discovered her son carrying Finn in his car seat.

"Mom?"

"Hey there. Damn, is it quittin' time already?" She glanced at her watch, surprised that it read half-past six. She took off a dirty glove and wiggled one of Finn's small tennis shoes. "Hello, sweet angel," she cooed, and as if hearing his grandmother's sing-song voice, the baby smiled, before shoving a wet fist into his mouth.

"She split," Matt blurted.

"What? Who split?" Dee asked, removing her other glove and work smock. She walked to the outdoor sink and washed her hands while looking at her son.

"Drea."

Dee paused in her rinsing and met Matthew's eyes with her own. "What do you mean she split?"

"I got home tonight, walked in, and Finn was screaming his head off."

She dried her hands, then moved to unstrap the baby from the car seat, bringing him to her chest, only to discover he needed a change, and quirked an eyebrow at her distracted son.

"Where was he?" She led him into her office and grabbed the portable changing table she kept in the closet and gestured for the baby bag.

"In his drawer," Matt said, referring to Finn's make-shift crib they fashioned out of a dresser drawer on the floor. He handed her the bag.

"Was he okay? How long was he there by himself?"

"Yeah, he's fine, just pissed. God knows for how long."

Dee let it go, as the proof of it laid on the table, peeing. "And why do you think she's not coming back?" Dee asked. "I mean, how do you know that? Maybe she…"

Matthew reached into his back pocket and took out some legal papers, which proved to relinquish all her rights as Finn's mother. He peeled off a yellow Post-It note, scrawled with a black marker, and read.

"Matt, I never wanted this. I'm going back and don't try to find me. When you get home, I'll be halfway to where I'm going next. It sucks. Sorry, Drea." He stopped and looked up from the note. "She didn't even say where she was going or anything."

Dee finished sprinkling some baby powder on her grandson, as her mind raced. At least she did them the favor of terminating her rights. *How and when did she meet with a lawyer?* She secured the tabs on the baby's disposable diaper, before pulling up his pants. They'd have to make sure the documents were legal. She'd stopped breast feeding on the second day, so that wouldn't be a problem. His face expressed genuine surprise at the situation. In one year's time, the couple met, created a child together, and the girl left, as if nothing between them occurred at all. Matt turned sixteen just the month before, and his eyes expressed hurt over the girl's betrayal because he believed in the fairy tale.

"Oh, Matthew." Dee hiked Finn onto her shoulder and walked to her son. She brought an arm around him and squeezed.

"What am I supposed to do now?"

"We'll figure it out, honey." She pulled back and gazed into the eyes, so much like her husband's. "It's better that you found this out now, Matty. If she left when he was older, it would've been a lot harder for Finn. He won't want for her, I promise."

"Mom, you don't understand."

"Yes, I do. You aren't the only one who lost a father young, Matthew. Your father passed when you were a year old. Mine died the day I was born."

"And you're saying that makes it easier?"

"Oh, hell, no. I'm just trying to tell you that your Kupuna was there for me. I tried to be there for you, maybe not as much as you needed, but I tried. And we'll both be here for Finn." She lifted a hand to his cheek. "And you'll be great at it because look how much you've grown up and changed over the last eight months. Look at what you've done, Matty." She acknowledged the baby.

"Yeah?" He placed a hand on Finn's back.

"Yeah," she chuckled. "What d'ya say we grab a pizza, go to the beach and come up with a game plan?"

"Okay," he said, relieved, and let out a shaky breath. "That sounds good."

CHAPTER 13

NOVEMBER 1982

THE PACIFIC HURRICANE SEASON of 1982 began in June, culminating in eleven tropical storms and twelve hurricanes. Reports of a large tropical storm approaching the Hawai'ian Islands blanketed the wires in mid-November. As the days progressed, the storm increased in severity and given the name, Hurricane IWA. The wind gusts exceeded one hundred miles per hour and contained seas of over thirty feet in height. It devastated parts of Oahu, the Forbidden Isle of Ni'ihau and the south beaches of Kaua'i at Po'ipū.

Dee stood amidst the ruins of the home her family inhabited for over forty years. Most of the physical mementos of her life gone, she moved the rest of her meager belongings into storage and set up interim housekeeping at the Cornucopia as the clean-up efforts began. During the hurricane, the Taylor family sheltered in a local school, with the rest of the local community, but Matthew's apartment, being so far inland, remained unscathed. Finn's father took on extra work with a local clean-up and re-building crew, named Hilo's Handyman most evenings and weekends, to help clean up and rebuild the island's most ravaged spots, while Dee took care of Finn and worked at the Cornucopia.

Matt found Dee dancing around the large cornucopia display with Finn when he got off work and chuckled. Life was going well. He and his mom bonded, united in raising Finn. He felt strong and that he'd conquered some demons, at last. Dee dipped a giggling Finn and noticed her son.

"There's Dada." Finn squealed in delight, so Dee dipped him again as Matthew walked over to him. "Dada." The baby blew spit bubbles and focused on his dad.

Matt took his son and held him up in the air, then brought him down for a hug, as Dee patted his back.

"How was your day?"

"Good. Busy."

"I'm almost done here, wanna grab some dinner?"

"Actually, I was hoping I could get you to watch him a little while longer. Lucas asked if I could help clear some rooms, at the King Kaumuali'i Condos. It's his highest-paying job right now, and the dumpsters are almost full. If we get the last few cleared, we can get it out of there sooner and be ready to go Monday.”

“Which means more profit?”

“Yeah, he said he’d give us bonuses.”

“Nice. Yes, I can definitely take the peanut.” She looked at her son’s tired face. “Burning the candle at both ends?”

“A little.”

“Okay, well, why don’t I take Mr. Finn tonight for the whole night and you do your work and get some sleep.”

“Really?”

“Absolutely.”

He grinned at her and kissed her cheek. “Thanks, Mom. I’ll try to get done early tomorrow.”

“Okay, well call the house first. I’m not sure what time I’m coming in tomorrow. Toni is still learning.”

“She the hot, new checkout girl?”

“Stop it.” Dee said in mock reproach, “You’ve got enough on your plate right now.”

He kissed her again, then his baby, and went back to work.

Lucas Kent, foreman for Hilo's, approached Matt as he picked up large piles of debris and heaved it into a large metal trash container.

"Hey kid," Kent called out and Matt turned to look at him.

"Hey, boss."

"Can you do me a favor and start on twelve with Clarkson and me?" The boss jerked a finger to his left, at a portly gentleman in his forties.

"Sure." Matt threw a palm tree branch into the container and followed the older men to the upper levels.

"Aw, man these fucking stairs." Carlson puffed like a steam engine. "I wished they'd get the elevator working."

Matt eyed the rather large ass wiggling its way up the stairs in front of him and smiled. "Naw, man, this is the way we get our exercise."

They reached the twelfth floor and Clarkson leaned on his knees and tried to catch his breath. "You work at the plantation during the week, don't ya?"

"Yeah."

"Christ, I wish I was your age again, kid."

Twelve-A, the hardest hit condo of the building, contained caved in walls, a collapsed ceiling and fallen beams throughout the apartment. The men cleared the area, and the room opened up.

"Oh, shit!" Matt looked down at the gash in his jeans. A large post fell out of the wall with several rusty nails sticking out down low. One tore through Matt's jeans and cut him on the shin. Not wanting anyone else to get hurt, Matthew withdrew his hammer and tried to pound the nails gently into the post. A precarious beam balanced on top of it fell onto his back and neck, dropping him to the floor. He screamed out in pain and tried to shove the beam off him to no avail. It felt like someone laid a hot wire in his spine, and he cried out again. At the sound, Clarkson and Kent ran over and removed the heavy object from his broken body.

"Call an ambulance," Lucas commanded, then turned back to his worker. "Hold on a minute, Matt, and lie still, don't twist. One of those nails gauged out a groove in your back."

"One got me in the leg too. Is it bad?"

"At very least you'll need a few stitches, and a tetanus shot. How ya feeling?"

"Like a human piñata." He grunted and tried to straighten to a more comfortable position, but pain radiated up his spine. "Ah, shit, man, something doesn't feel right in my back."

"It's okay, just hold still, and we'll get ya to the hospital."

When the medics arrived, they strapped Matthew onto a spine board, securing his head as they evacuated him down the stairs and loaded him into an ambulance, He asked for someone to call his mother, and by the time Dee arrived, he'd already been told he fractured two of his vertebra and might require surgery.

"Matt!" She held onto his hand and moved into his field of vision. "Oh my God, are you all right?"

"Where's Finn?"

"He's with Toni."

"The hottie?"

"Yeah," Dee chuckled. "He's okay. What about you? What did they say?"

"He said they'll try a brace first, and if it doesn't heal the way it's supposed to, he'll fuse two of the vertebrae together."

"What about your spinal cord?"

"Said it was all good or intact or something." Matthew winced in pain.

"Bad?"

"Hurts like a motherfucker."

"Have they given you anything?"

"If they have, but it hasn't kicked in yet."

"Be careful with the pain meds, Matty. They're so addictive."

"Yeah, I asked the doctor about it." He gasped as pain coursed through him, and he tried yet again to get more comfortable without moving too much. "He said there's been a letter published or something about this new med they're giving me. He said it has a lower chance at becoming addicted to it, when pain is chronic or long term or something."

"Okay, what's it called?"

"OxyContin."

In the months that followed the hurricane, Dee found competent builders to design her new home. She continued to live at the Cornucopia with Finn, while Matthew, unable to pick up his son, started physical therapy for his back. He couldn't return to his lucrative but highly physical job at the plantation for the foreseeable future, so it relieved them both when Worker's Compensation covered most of the costly expenses.

However, Matt's life, once filled with direction and purpose, gave way to desolation and self-pity, and he craved the oblivion the new drug prescribed to him provided. Concerned he would slide backward, Dee questioned how long he needed to be on the OxyContin, and the doctor assured her it wouldn't be much longer. Once his back healed to the point he could resume his role as custodian of his son, the doctor discontinued the drug.

Dee started construction on her house and business. The work distracted her with a million decisions and directions. Contractors and the physical labors of her business occupied her days, while payroll and bookkeeping consumed her nights. Most evenings she fell asleep with her head on the kitchen table and only spoke with Matthew and Finn by phone, though they stopped by twice to see the progress.

After several weeks, she discovered she missed them, and picked up some food to surprise them with at their apartment. When her second knock elicited no response, she frowned and tried the door, finding it unlocked.

"Matthew?" she called out into the dreary apartment.

Sitting in his playpen watching cartoons, with several half-eaten chocolate chip cookies strewn around him, Finn turned and grinned at his grandmother.

"Thee, Thee, Thee," he squealed, and tried to pull himself to standing.

"Good boy," she cooed, and when he stood and reached out his chubby arms, she picked him up. "Duh, Duh, Dee," his grandmother sounded out.

"Thee, Thee," Finn bounced in her arms and pressed sticky hands to her face, before giving her an equally sticky kiss.

"Where's Dada?"

"Da," he answered, and pointed toward the kitchen.

"Dada's in the kitchen?" she responded and glanced around the messy apartment. Smelling the baby's messy diaper, she said, "Whew-ee, you need a change, little man."

Matt had done an outstanding job at creating a clean, somewhat furnished home for his son and himself. Dee drew her brows together now as she stepped over trash, traversing toward the kitchen. Heaps of messy dishes containing a green fuzzy mold on the top of the half-eaten food laid on every available surface. *What the hell's going on? He's going to get rats.*

"Matthew?" she called out but received no response. She retraced her steps into the compact living room and approached the bedroom door. Rapping on it, she called out, "Matt?" When he grunted, she opened the door, and the stench of old food, stale air and unwashed male, assaulted her. "Ew! It stinks like a dead rhino's ass in here." She flicked on the light.

"Shit, Ma!"

Dee scanned the room of beer cans, clothes, trash and an open container of pills on his nightstand, then at her rumpled son. Eyes turned into slits, his mouth hung open at an unbecoming angle, higher than a kite.

"Matthew? What the hell's going on here?"

"Da," Finn chortled and wiggled to get down.

She secured her arms around the baby and stomped over to her son's nightstand, snatching up the bottle and scanning the prescription label. "I thought you were done with these." She glared at her son. "Matt?"

"It's fine," he insisted with exasperation. "I just re-tweaked my back."

"Since when? You never said anything, I would have come and helped. Look at all this. Matty… You can't leave the top off this. If Finn ate one of these, he'd die." At a loss, she scanned the room again. "How long have you been in bed?" The toddler reached out a hand to grab at the bottle, and she held it away from him. "No, no! That's yucky. Icky!"

Finn blew a raspberry.

"Dee, I said, I'm good. We're good. What are you doing here, anyway?"

"What am I doing here? I haven't seen you guys in weeks. I thought I'd bring you some food, but I'm not eating in this disease-laden apartment. Come on, let's go down to the beach."

"I don't wanna go to the beach."

"You're going. Come on, it's beautiful outside. Finn's out there eating cookies."

"I know. I gave them to him."

Trying to keep her cool, Dee drew in a deep breath. "How about I take Finn for the night? It'll give you some time to clean the place up."

"Fine," her son snapped, throwing off the covers. "We'll go to the Goddamn beach."

The fresh air and sunshine seemed to soften the tension, as Finn played in the sand, and Dee tried to talk to her son.

"Honey, what's going on? You said those pills were supposed to be less addictive."

"They are, you even heard the doctor say so with your own ears. So, just chill." He breathed in and out, almost in an exhausted pant, then looked at her face. "Look, I'm just in pain, Mom, it'll pass." He stared out at the ocean with wistful longing. "I wanna go surfin' again."

"Let's try tomorrow."

"I can't… I got PT."

"Okay, well, I can watch Finn for you. It's been a while since I've gotten to hang out with him." *And I can clean up your pigsty.*

"Okay, I'll bring him…"

"No, I'll come to your place. When you go, I want you to ask them about weaning yourself off those damn pills. I noticed you're drinking again, too. How long's that been going on?"

"Last night." When she only stared at him, he added, "It was a hard day Jesus. Back off."

"You need to go to a meeting, Matt… tonight if possible. You aren't acting like yourself and backsliding. Don't forget you've got a great thing going here."

"Look, don't tell me what I got. I know what I got." He glanced at her worried face, then at his son who brought a shell to him and smiled. "Thanks, buddy."

"Bee, Bee, Bee," the baby chanted and dropped onto his butt, then handed his grandmother a shell too. It brought tears to her eyes, and Matt saw it.

"Mom, it's okay, stop worrying. Look, I'll go to a meeting, I promise. Everything's cool."

"You deserve to be happy, Matt. You deserve that little boy, and he deserves a clean father who will love him and take care of him."

"I know."

They finished their meal and when Dee returned in the morning, she brought her own clean playpen to the apartment and set it up in the kitchen near the screened patio door. She set to work washing dishes, doing laundry, changing sheets and scrubbing the tiny bathroom. When Finn wanted to play, she played, then would set him down for a nap or quiet play-time and go back to polishing floors and scrubbing down cupboards. The duo purchased groceries and supplies for both the refrigerator and pantry, and by the time Matthew returned, he seemed more relaxed, and at peace.

"Wow, place looks great." he noted. "You didn't have to do that."

"Yes, I did." She sighed. "Look, I know when I'm bummed out and overwhelmed it's easy to stay in the pit. Real easy, but we gotta stay in the light, Matt."

"Yeah," he agreed and nuzzled his son's neck, breathing him in. "I will."

CHAPTER 14

MAY 1984

THE NEXT TIME DEE went to Matt's place, Evan sat on his couch, with Finn on his lap, grinning at her. "Hey, Mrs. T. Long time, no see."

Dee blanched. "Where's Matt?"

A woman in a skimpy dress walked out of her son's room and sat down next to Evan. She gave Dee a bored, "Hey."

Dee walked over to Evan and grabbed Finn from him. "Where's my son?"

"I think he went over to Queen's Bath for some cliff jumping." He nodded at the woman. "Me and Desiree are stayin' here a few days with him."

"Like hell you are."

"Christ, you haven't changed a bit, have you? We're watching the kid until he gets back, which should be any minute."

"I'll take him home with me."

"Like hell you will. I don't know if Matt even talks to you, crazy bitch. That kid ain't leavin' here."

Dee clutched the baby and looked around the apartment. She didn't have her glasses on, but it looked like a needle and spoon laid on the kitchen table. Not sure what to do, she glanced back at Evan, who grinned at her with malice. The door burst opened, and Matt walked in gesturing as he talked.

"Hey, that was so cool," he said to Evan. "Alex almost bought it on the rocks but.."

"Dude, your ole lady's here."

Matt glanced at where his friend pointed saw his mother. "Oh, hey, Mom."

Breathing heavily, she stared daggers at him. "Matthew, what in the hell is going on, here?" He walked over to her and reached out his hands for Finn. The baby saw his Dad and squirmed to reach him. Dee clutched him tighter to her, and Matt narrowed his eyes at her.

"Come here, bud." He took Finn from her arms, and Dee saw his eyes were clear, but she did smell alcohol on his breath.

"You've been drinking."

"Yeah, but I wasn't driving." He grinned. "What are you doing here?"

"I was worried."

"When aren't you worried?"

Evan laughed. "Well, clearly all is good in paradise. Come on, Finn, let's go. Me and Desiree are hungry for fish tacos."

"Here," Dee suggested, "Why don't I take Finn with me? You guys can all go hang out." She reached out for him, but Matt turned him away from her.

"No, he's good. Look, Mom, I've got people over. You should've called."

"Matt…"

"I'll call you tomorrow." Evan light a cigarette for himself and Desiree and the small space filled with smoke.

"Matt, it's not good for the baby to be in a room full of smoke. Here I'll take him, and you guys have fun."

"Evan, go open a window or better yet stand out on the back patio, that's what I do when I want a smoke." Evan rolled his eyes but moved toward the kitchen. "Bye, Dee. Nice seein' ya."

Matt walked to the front door and opened it. "I'll talk to you tomorrow, Mom."

Dee wanted to cry. Everything inside her said to take Finn and run, but she didn't have any rights. She walked through the door, then turned to her son.

"You are scaring me."

"Sound like you got a problem, then." The room erupted in laughter, and Dee's eyes filled with tears, and he closed the door on them.

✳

"Hello, Mrs. Locke. It's nice to meet you." Dee shook hands and smiled across the desk at the social worker her lawyer recommended at the child welfare office.

"Oh, please call me, Lola." The woman grinned at Dee. "What a fantastic dress."

"Oh… thank you," Dee looked down at the large purple hibiscus flowers dotting along the lime green base. "I dress for me."

"I wouldn't have it any other way, Mrs. Taylor."

"And you can call me Dee."

"Dee it is. Okay, well I've reviewed all the notes here, and you're searching for some information about getting custody and maybe adopting your grandson, Finn, is that correct?" Hearing it spoken out loud caused a spasm of pain in Dee's gut, and Lola smiled in sympathy at her.

"Yes," Dee murmured. "I don't know what to do or where to start, or even how far to take it. I just know something has to happen for Finn's sake, and I was hoping you could help us."

"Well, why don't you tell me what's going on, in your own words, and we'll see what we can do."

Dee told her everything. The path her son traveled, his upbringing, her mistakes, and only stopped to answer the social worker's questions. "Today it looked like there may have been a needle on the table, but I didn't have my glasses on and I could tell for sure. If it was, he may be back on heroin."

"Okay," Lola said and reached a hand across to Dee's. "Well, first off, how did he seem?"

"He'd had a drink or two, but wasn't drunk."

"Were his eyes clear?"

"Yes."

"Do you think the baby is in danger?"

"Well, I don't trust his friends or anything. He wasn't high in that exact moment, but I'm sure he's using again. It's exactly how he acted before."

"Okay, we'll send a car over and check it out." Lola made the call and when she finished, turned back to Dee. "Okay, they'll do a check and call me back. I'm sorry, Dee. You and your family have been on a hard road here. There's been a lot of loss, and can I just ask how *you're* doing?"

Dee blinked at her and tried to remember the last time someone asked her that. "Oh, I'm okay," she answered in weary resolve. "I just have to stop this cycle, for Finn's sake. Yes, we lost Mama. I lost my dad, Matthew lost his dad, and it's awful, but if things don't get fixed, Finn will lose his father, too."

"Would you be willing to get some counseling? Maybe work through all these feelings of anger and loss?"

"I'm not angry."

"Aren't you?"

Anger? Disappointment, yes, but anger? She closed her eyes and turned her head toward the wall for a moment. If Arthur hadn't died, how different would things be now? Would his simple presence have saved their son? Tears sprang to her eyes as the realization hit her. The day she lost Arthur, the fates damned them all. It *would not* bleed into Finn.

"I'll go. If it'll help Finn and Matthew, I'll do damn near anything. Do you require it for custody?"

"No, not necessarily." Lola reached across the desk to grasp her hand again. "I'm not telling you to go. It's just… you've been through a lot and there will be more to go through yet, for you, Finn and your son. I think it could be beneficial for all of you, as you put it, for stopping the cycle."

"Okay, I promise you I'll give it the consideration it deserves, but right now my primary concern is for my grandson." She contemplated the kind, light summer blue eyes of the woman across from her. "Look, I don't like to ask for help… but I need it. I need it like I've never needed it before… please, Lola."

"Okay," the social worker said with decision and patted Dee's hands, before turning to a drawer in her desk and withdrawing several papers from different folders. "We have some paperwork to fill out, and we need to set up a home visit."

"What's that?"

"It's where we come to the house and make sure you're set up is all safe for Mr. Finn."

"Does he need to have his own room?" Dee asked, worried. "The hurricane destroyed my house, and we're getting there, but we aren't quite finished with everything yet."

"Are you on the south side? Where are you living now?"

"I own Dee's Cornucopia."

"Oh, I love that place. I go there all the time."

Dee smiled. "Well, it came with a house on it and we converted that into a gift shop and office. I turned one room back into a bedroom for myself, after the hurricane. It's got a kitchen and a bathroom and everything, but I can clear out another room to make sure Finn has his own space, if we need to. It's temporary. The house should be ready in a month."

"No, it should be fine. Just make sure he has a bed, and that everything's child-proofed."

"Okay, then what?"

"We'll begin by doing a health screening and deter-mine if your income can support you and Finn both. There'll be a background check, and we'll need some references."

"How long will all that take?"

"It can take between two or three months for everything to process."

"Two or three months?" Dee asked, concerned. "But Finn…"

"That's for you to become a legal foster parent. If we find Finn endangered, which with the home environment and medications you describe seems to be the case, we can ask a judge for emergency temporary custody."

"Okay, and how long will that take?"

"It depends on the judge and his docket, or schedule. My hope is less than a week. That's the best-case scenario. The judge will hear the arguments and you and your son will be there. If he feels Finn's not safe, he could remove him from the home that day. In fact, he wouldn't go back until we deemed the apartment safe." Lola scanned Dee's face. "So, give me a day to get things organized, and get the home study done. It could be as early as tomorrow, but don't hold your breath." The phone rang, and Lola answered.

"Lola Locke." She listened, then depressed the speakerphone button. "Hi, what's going on over there?"

"Hey Lola, it's Officer Kinney. I went by Matthew Taylor's apartment. I have some history with the family." Dee smiled. She'd heard he was married with a baby of his own now, but the officer didn't hold Dee's reasoning for not getting involved with each other against her. Years passed since she last heard his voice and knowing he was the officer in charge made her relax.

"Hi Marshall, it's Dee."

"Dee. Hello. He wasn't there. No one was. I checked everything, and it's all secure. I knocked on a neighbor's door and he said he thought they were all going away for the weekend."

"Going where?"

"He didn't say. I'll spread the word to keep an eye out, though. Most of the guys here know Matt." Dee sighed and closed her eyes. "From before, or is it a recent thing?"

"I'm sorry, but recently. He's created a couple of disturbances at some bars, and someone accused him of stealing from the till, but they couldn't prove it. They don't have a camera, but they're pretty good people, Dee. They wouldn't accuse someone of something like that if they didn't believe he'd done it."

"Till? He's working somewhere?"

"I guess Tiki Tahiti sometimes, and no, not anymore. They fired him, three days ago." He paused as if thinking about what to say next. "Look, I'm glad you're taking the next steps for your grandson's sake. We'll keep an eye out, okay? He'll show up."

Dee's eyes filled at so many lost opportunities. "Thank you." Lola hung up the phone, reached over and took Dee's hand.

"All right. We'll get the paperwork done and get you into the system and I'll try to schedule that date with the judge." Dee nodded and took a bittersweet but relieving breath in before letting it back out slow.

"Okay, then I'll go home and get things ready. So, you can come by whenever you want."

"Dee?"

"Yes?" She sat in her office going over a large order that needed to go out the following day, and making every effort to concentrate on it, when her intercom buzzed.

"Lola Locke on the phone."

Dee's head jerked up. "Okay, thanks." She switched lines before answering the phone. "Lola, how are you?" She stood and walked around her desk.

"I'm great, ready for the weekend."

"Are you going somewhere?"

"Yes, as a matter a fact, I'm meeting my hubby, Randy, at the airport and we're going to Oahu for the weekend. It's our tenth anniversary."

"Oh." Dee's heart sank, believing they would place the case on hold until the woman came back. Two days, and she still hadn't heard from Matt.

"But, not to worry, if you have questions, just call and either Sarah Gregory or Gloria Coyle, the other social workers here, and they will be happy to help."

"Okay, thank you."

She moved back around the desk, getting ready to hang up, when Lola said, "We have a date. Are you ready?"

"Oh! Ah." Dee grabbed a pen and, not seeing any scratch paper, wrote the date in one week's time on her arm. After thanking Lola, she sat at her desk, eyes falling on a photo of Matthew, holding his son, and standing in the ocean smiling back at her. Overwhelmed with sadness that their lives came to this, her gut tightened. However, Finn's safety came first, and then they would tackle Matthew's addiction.

A knock sounded at her door, and she turned to open it. Toni stood before her, saying they needed her out front. Dee acknowledged her and glanced one more time at the picture, before she locked her door and walked down the hall. As she rounded the corner to the main gift shop, two police officers stood looming. She stepped back as Marshall turned around.

"Hi, Dee," he said, voice full of sympathy, and extended a hand.

"Marshall." She exhaled and shook his hand, then leaned against the counter, shaking her head in frustration. "What did he do?"

"Dee… I'm sorry to have to tell you this, but he was found a few hours ago at the base of Kipu Falls." The officer hesitated, then murmured, "He's gone."

Time paused, and her vision narrowed. "Gone?" she asked, a greasy panic rising in her gut. "Wait… what?" She raised a hand to her mouth and noticed Toni's head jerk up.

"We think he drowned." Marshall cleared his throat. "Some of his, ah, friends, came forward." He hesitated, considering her face, then averted his eyes. "It seems they were doing some partying and cliff diving off the rocks out there. He -ah- he jumped off and -well- you know what it's like out there. It brought him down hard into the rocks. His friends got him out of the water and onto the path, but they got scared and left. Some tourists went down there to see the falls and found him." The full ramifications started to make themselves known. "About the same time those friends came into the station to tell us what happened."

"When did this happen?" she whispered, trying to calculate time.

"I guess it was two nights ago. Look, Dee…"

"Oh God!" she screamed. "Where's Finn? My grandson, Finn, he's just a baby and I…"

"Dee. Dee! He's safe," the officer cooed. "We think he was there that first night and they gave him something to sleep. So, we didn't hear him. He's a little dehydrated, but safe. Some neighbors called it in. It seems they heard the boy crying and broke in to find out what was going on, about the same time we got the call about Kipu Falls."

"Where's Finn now?"

"The hospital. Child welfare services here on..."

"Just... just please don't do anything, Marshall. Please..."

No longer able to think of her son, Dee only wanted to go to the best part of him. She ran back to her room and fumbled with the keys to unlock the door. However, her hands shook with such violence, she couldn't make the key and lock merge. Officer Kinney walked to her and withdrew them from her hand. The sizeable man took her in his arms as overwhelming pain bubbled through her entire being, consuming her. Her body convulsed with an effort to hold it in.

"Shh, take a moment and breathe, honey," he whispered in her ear. "It will be all right, Dee. You are a strong woman."

He patted her back as she keened out all the years of grief and heartache. She didn't know how long he held her for, but she slowly returned to herself, and he finally let her go. Kinney turned to unlock her door, saying, "Get your things, and I'll take you to the boy, then I'll bring you home when you're ready."

She ran into the hospital where her frightened and wailing grandson sat up in a hospital bed with

IV fluids running from a bag into his tiny fist and wrapped in several layers of bandage to keep it in place. At a nod from the doctor, she picked him up and drew him close to her. The baby calmed into hiccups. He settled his extraordinary eyes on his grandmother's, and she kissed both of his wet cheeks, then he kissed hers in return.

"It's all right, baby. Grandma's got you." She bounced him up and down, patting his back. "Shh, it's okay, Finn. I'm never gonna let you go," her voice broke. "I promise."

Finn stayed the night for observation and fell asleep exhausted in his grandmother's arms. Around ten that night, the physician came into the room to check on him, and after making all the observations and reading the baby's vitals, turned to face Dee.

"Mrs. Taylor… Your son's downstairs. At some point we'll need you to make a positive I.D. and sign some paperwork, but only when you're ready."

Finn remained asleep on her chest. *Christ, please don't make me do this. Please don't make me see him that way.* She glanced back at the doctor, but she knew it was pointless. Sooner or later, she'd have to face it.

"Okay." She leaned back and glanced down at her grandson. "He's pretty out. I don't want to go down there with him awake, and I sure as hell aren't bringing him with me. Let's just go now, if he stays asleep." Almost wishing the boy would wake up, she laid Finn

down in his crib and watched to make sure he continued to sleep. Finn made a small gurgle, then worked
the pacifier in his mouth again.

They walked down the hallway of white walls and
the smell of antiseptic in silence. When they reached
the morgue, the doctor introduced her to the Medical
Examiner who requested identification before he left
to retrieve her son. After fifteen minutes, the M.E.
escorted her into a cold, sterile room. The minty green
walls, bright fluorescent lights, and drain in the floor
reeked of death and despair. A sinister stainless-steel
table, with a sheet over the broken shell of her son
stood amidst terrifying equipment and instruments.
Dee stopped and gasped, not sure if she believed
the reality of the situation until just then. The M.E.
stopped and observed her, not without sympathy.

"Take your time, Mrs. Taylor." He walked over and
stood in front of her. "Let me just explain what you're
about to see, okay?"

Shaking, she nodded, pressing her lips together in a
gutted frown, then taking a deep breath, she captured
the physician's gaze with her own. As he spoke of
bloating, color, and injuries of the body, Dee's mind
became numb and raised a fist to her mouth. Terrified
to see her son that way, she trembled, but as he lifted
the blanket… he was simply the baby she and Arthur
created. Though trauma occurred from hitting the
rocks, Matthew's relaxed face almost smiled in peace.

She didn't hear the doctor say he'd give her some time, she just stood alone in the room with her son. Dee reached out a hand and stroked his cold cheek.

"Oh baby…" Her words echoed throughout the room. "Matthew?" Tears rolled down her face and her nose ran unheeded. "I am so, so sorry, my sweet boy." She could almost feel his presence in the room. "God, how I wish…" She stroked his hair back. "I should have been better for you. I wish I could have done more." She laid a hand on his chest, then gasped at the utter stillness of his body. "I won't fail you with Finn. I promise you with everything I am, I'll take care of him, Matty. Whatever it takes." She sniffed, loud and wet, and closed her eyes.

Dee floated between that space of dreams yet remained awake. Smoke swirled in her mind and through the mist walked four souls - her father, Arthur, Catherine, and holding her husband and mother's hand, Matthew. She didn't know who to look at first, afraid to take her eyes off one in fear of the others disappearing. For a moment, she wanted to be with them, but Matthew shook his head.

"Matty." Dee cried and reached out to him.

"I'm so sorry, Mama," he whispered. "For everything. I didn't want this to happen, I just couldn't cut it loose."

"We have him, darling," Catherine reassured her daughter and smiled over at Matt with love, which he returned. "He'll be all right."

"I don't understand why you all left me," Dee choked out on a sob.

"We haven't left you, sweetheart," her father said. Dee studied his face. So much of herself reflected in the eyes and mouth.

"Okay, fine, yes, you're always with me, right?" Dee snapped. "Just watching me from above or some other bullshit."

"No, Mama, I'm in Finn," her son replied and vanished.

"I'm in the garden, my sweetest heart," her mother grinned, touched her heart, and evaporated.

"I have never left *you*." George walked to her and placed an icy hand upon her chest. "We walk with you every step of the way." He disappeared and the icy palm print lingered a moment before it, too, vanished.

Dee looked at Arthur, helpless and resigned. "It doesn't help. I know that, darlin'," he said in his soft Alabama drawl, and took a step closer to her.

"I messed it all up without you."

"No, you didn't," he chided and stroked her cheek. "So much is coming your way, my little dove, and you need to let us go," he warned in a gentle voice. "Can you do that for me, honey? Be happy and just live? You and Finn?" She gave a reluctant nod, tears dripping off her jawline.

"I'm so lonely, Arthur… so scared."

"You won't be anymore, honey."

"He has your eyes, ya know," Dee murmured. "Finn."

"I know… I gave them to him when we met here," he whispered and faded. "I wanted you to recognize me when you saw them and know I'm always with you." Arthur, almost transparent, spoke his last words. "I will always love you, my sassy, sassy dove." And in the next moment, he vanished into the ether.

EPILOGUE

AUGUST 1995

D EE PULLED INTO THE driveway of her home and walked around to the back of her car to collect the groceries from within. She glanced up at the brick house she'd lived in for over a decade with Finn and smiled. The brick house and concrete bulkhead of both her home and the Cornucopia, especially after Iniki, the category four Hurricane that landed the year prior, proved to be her best investment yet. The fifty-three-year-old, her thirteen-year-old grandson, and all their property on Po'ipū survived.

She entered the domicile and laid the bags of groceries on the kitchen counter. The open dishwasher revealed one bowl inside it, still dripping with milk, and she smiled.

"Hey, wanna go surfin'?" she called out to Finn. "We got a few more hours before sunset."

"Yeah," Finn yelled with enthusiasm, and the pounding of his feet resounded through the floorboards. He skidded around the corner clad only in a purple sock and bright orange board shorts. He flung a book on the counter and sprinted toward the front door, on a mission for the garage, calling, "I gotta get my board, though."

Already several inches taller than Dee, the boy showed the promise of the man he would become. Dee grinned and caught him around his skinny waist before he flew by her. She hugged him to her from behind.

"Thank you for putting your dishes away, love."

"I know, you always say that." He giggled and reached up to her hat to retrieve three fat grapes from it, then popped them into his mouth.

"Well, I always appreciate it." She kissed the back of his head, "I love you, kid."

"Love you too."

She squeezed him tight, then let him go, and he jolted forward, as if on a spring. He glanced back and smiled Matthew's smile. In fact, Finn possessed the best traits of all of them. Her father's strength, her mother's kindness, Arthur's generosity and her precociousness. Dee imagined he would move into more challenging times as a teenager, but also understood without a doubt they'd be okay.

He enjoyed calling her Dee, saving Grandma for times of injury or deep emotion, and their everlasting bond cemented that first day in the hospital. Throughout the years she'd been honest about his father, telling him both the good and the bad, but also letting him know how much fatherhood changed Matt, and how much he loved his son. Dee believed if Matthew had just a few more years to mature, he would've made it to the other side and been an amazing father to his son. *After all, I'm a much better mother the second time around.*

"Did you get bagels?"

She pulled them out of the shopping bag, along with a tub of cream cheese, and wiggled them. "Even got pineapple cream cheese for you."

"Yes!"

Chuckling, she put away the few perishables from the grocery bags and noticed the thin book the boy threw on the counter. She turned it toward her. Splashed across the cover, an adorable Hawai'ian Monk seal grinned back at her.

"What's this?" Dee asked, holding it up as the boy ran back into the house and let the screen door snap back with a bang.

"Oh, Ray and me…"

"Ray and I."

"Yeah, Ray and I talked with a guy on the beach today, he was like giving the seals some medicine and testing them and stuff."

"Testing them?"

"Yeah," Finn became animated "It was so cool, he said sometimes the seals get parasite and they take samples to make sure they're okay."

"Oh yeah?"

"Uh-huh." Finn spun around, grabbed his flip flops from a shoe cubby and threw them on the tiled floor. He stripped off his sock and slid each foot into a sandal. "And then he spent like an entire hour telling us all about them. He's a marine biologist."

"Oh, that's cool," Dee said.

"Yeah. That's what I want to do," he said in all seriousness. "When I grow up, I'm gonna be a marine biologist. They even have programs on Oahu, I looked it up on the computer at the library today."

"Ray gonna do that too?"

"No, he said he wants to surf all day. I told him to go bigger."

"Bigger?"

"Yeah, he's really good at like drawing stuff."

"Well, I think you'd be a fantastic marine biologist. All those times we go to the tide pools and I have to drag you away… you're a natural."

"Yeah." He ran over to her and gave her another hug. "Thanks, Grandma. I love you."

"I love you, too. Will you put my board on the car too? I'll be right there… I just need to turn off the sprinklers in the backyard."

"Okay." He sprinted back toward the garage again and she chuckled, shaking her head.

Walking over to the slider, she opened the door and stepped out onto the patio. The middle of summer sparkled all around her and the beautiful gardens blossomed into vibrant displays. Nothing in her life presented monochromatically anymore, instead it promised a vivaciousness, as colorful as her cornucopia display. She stooped over and twisted the water faucet handle off, then turned to re-enter the house when something about the sea pulled at her.

Turning, the sun beamed its light through a large water funnel that gyrated across the ocean with slow purpose. She closed her eyes, like she always did, and sensed the warmth of the energy flood through her. She smiled, and when she opened her eyes again, something in her periphery caught her attention. Turning, the most beautiful woman Dee had ever seen stood in the middle of her flower bed with a hand on the old banyan tree. The vision picked one of her plumeria blossoms and placed it behind her ear and into her long golden-brown hair.

"Hey!" Dee called, taking a step toward the woman. "Who are you? What are you doing back here?"

"Demeter."

"Ah, no, it's Deidre… Dee, actually… Do I know you?" When the woman continued to gaze at her, Dee said, "Look here now, you shouldn't be back there. You need to skedaddle."

"Time draws near." The woman observed Dee with love and adoration in her eyes.

"What?" Something in her memory sparked. *Am I wrong? Have I seen her before?* She wanted to ask, but the woman spoke again.

"We *will* meet again."

In the time it took Dee to blink, the woman vanished. Dee scanned the area and blinked hard a few more times, but she didn't see the woman anywhere. Her car's horn honked, and she gave a brief shake of her head, deciding she dreamed it. Thinking of the strange woman's last words, Dee said out loud, "Not bloody likely." Then ran out to meet her significant piece of immortality.

<h2 style="text-align:center">ACKNOWLEDGEMENTS</h2>

’D LIKE TO THANK and acknowledge a cornucopia of folks for their help with this novella.

First, Celtic Butterfly Publishing, for taking a chance on someone writing a story that spans a lifetime. These tales aren't the easiest to write, let alone publish in a novella. Thank you for your belief in me and Dee's beautiful story.

To my friend and assistant, Andrea Florescu, for doing all the things I don't like doing. I was blessed when you entered my life last year in the middle of a pandemic and helped me navigate a different way of reaching my readers. Thank you for your hours and hours of hard work, expertise and forcing me to point a few toes out of my comfort zone.

Judy Thomas, from Goddess Fish Promotions, thank you for taking on this project to edit, and helping me make this story the best it could be, as well as promoting my tales over the past couple of years.

A huge thank you to Dee's Cornucopia cover designer, Steven Novak at www.novakillustration.com I love the elements you used to create this beautiful work of art.

I'd like to give a shout out to Daniel Martinez, Chief Historian for the Pearl Harbor National Memorial, on Oahu, in Hawai'i. I know I couldn't keep a lot of the things we discussed in Dee's Cornucopia, but I will never forget the real stories you told me about the "day of that lives in infamy." Thank you for helping me with locations, timing and wording, and for all you do to keep December 7th and what happened that day, alive. I'm truly humbled by the picture you painted about what all those brave service men and women, their families and the citizens had to endure, and not Hollywood's romantic notion of it.

To Lihue Social Services Department, on Kaua'i, in Hawai'i. I truly appreciate the specifics you shared in regard to family services and capabilities in this referenced time period. As well as information on the hurricanes Iwa and Iniki. Your information was so incredibly helpful.

To the National Parks Service of Hawaii. Thank you for your expertise on the plantations and mills of this time. As well as the history of Kauai in the 1950's and 1960's, the information was invaluable.

A huge thank you to Grove Farm, and the Sugar Plantation Museum, on Kaua'i, in Hawai'i, for perfectly illustrating the life of a field hand on a sugar plantation. I loved the history, the Wilcox family, the train, the remnants of the period and the incredibly hardworking individuals it took to keep this historic site working for 150 glorious years. It's a true shame Hawai'i's once lucrative industry is, alas, no more.

To my beautiful auntie, Lola Locke, who helped me understand a very hard and private world and the process of family adoption. As well as individuals who wish to remain anonymous regarding the effects of drugs and alcoholism on a family unit. I can't thank you for trusting me with not only painful times in your lives but also for your openness and candor about tough love, family dysfunction and how it affects the children.

I was born on December 6th, and according to my father, I was the calm before the storm, although he probably thinks differently on that now. I always wanted to write a story about this time period. I loved reading the stories my grandparents wrote about their lives during this time, as well as hearing their endless tales growing up. They always had a magical quality to them that I don't think my generation or the generations after, can fully appreciate. The sense of true patriotism, sacrifice and really hard work, without the creature comforts of our cushy modern lives. I'd like to thank my parents, and grandparents and the beloved elders of our world for helping me to understand them, the truest and greatest generation. Please write your stories down, the good, the bad and the ugly, for we truly have so much to learn from you.

Finally thank you to my truest support system, Jeff, Paisley, Charlie, Nic, Jess, Natalie, Sarah, Debbie and Jeff. Your love and support, hugs and well wishes make my life so complete. Love you all!

JENY HECKMAN IS THE award-winning Paranormal and Fantasy Romance author of the Heaven & Earth series. Since her series debut in 2018, Jeny has captured the imagination and inspired the journey of readers worldwide.

Volume one, the Sea Archer, received the esteemed, "Best in Category" award from the 2018 Chanticleer International Book Awards for Paranormal Romance. Two years later, the Warrior's Progeny also won "Best in Category" from the Chanticleer International Book Awards for the Fantasy Romance genre, as well as earned the Crown Heart of Excellence from InD'Tale magazine. Her standalone Women's Fiction novel, entitled Releasing the Catch, was a finalist in the Feathered Quill awards, likewise received in 2020.

Jeny loves working with her charities, which include Hospice of the Northwest, the Michael J. Fox Parkinson's Foundation, the Seattle Children's Hospital and the American Cancer Society. Jeny lives in the Pacific Northwest with her husband of over twenty-eight years.

Thank you, for purchasing this publication
of Celtic Butterfly Publishing,

www.celticbutterflypublishing.com.

For questions or more information, contact
us at info@celticbutterflypublishing.com

**For more information on Jeny Heckman,
please follow her on social media**

Website: https://jenyheckman.com/

Facebook: https://bit.ly/3myAmm4

Twitter: https://bit.ly/3mwJ3wV

Instagram: https://bit.ly/3s5ypym

LinkedIn: https://bit.ly/2PFGAVe

Pinterest: https://bit.ly/3rWwHiU

GoodReads: https://bit.ly/3fd8RJA

BookBub: https://bit.ly/3sYOkzQ

YouTube: https://bit.ly/3ovNfUI

Newsletter: https://bit.ly/3wAZzkp

Podcast:

Anchor: https://bit.ly/3mxwQZo

Breaker: https://bit.ly/2PFH2mo

Pocket Casts: https://bit.ly/3t2mzXj

Radio Public: https://bit.ly/31WHSh5

Spotify: https://spoti.fi/3cZhiKr

An Excerpt

The Sea Archer: Book One

The Heaven & Earth Series

by Jeny Heckman

Published by the Wild Rose Press, 2018

CHAPTER 1

R AVEN SAT ON HER plush white couch, knees drawn up to her chin, clad in periwinkle pajamas and fuzzy pink socks. She had turned the couch from the center of the living room so that it faced the large floor-to-ceiling windows overlooking Puget Sound. When she reached for the box of tissues, she discovered it was empty, and her frown deepened. Looking over at the linen squares Donovan insisted should be there, Raven rolled her eyes. She remembered him saying only Philistines would lower themselves to use paper tissues. Rolling her eyes again, she stood up. Who even talks like that, she thought wearily. Deciding maybe wine and chocolate were needed more, she dabbed her watery nose on her sleeve and proceeded farther into the condo.

The kitchen was unblemished, with its frigid, white-walled tile and marble countertops. Reaching for the cupboard where she hid her stash of chocolate, Raven's eyes danced across the photo of her goddaughter Abby, taped on the door of her stainless-steel refrigerator. She sniffed and smiled. Abby was caught in mid belly-laugh the summer before when she popped up from the slip 'n slide in her backyard. Donovan would never have allowed the photo to be placed there, let alone taped to such an unforgiving surface. Raven didn't even remember putting it there after he left. She looked into the cupboard and discovered there was no more chocolate either.

"Fuck!" she stated emphatically. Staring into the near empty cupboard, she tried to will her dark- chocolate, salted-caramels into existence but to no avail. Screw it, she thought irritated, all I really need is the wine.

Using one of Donovan's fancy bottle openers, she tried to attach it to an unopened bottle. After two full minutes of trial and error, Raven poured the contents, more than socially acceptable, into a large crystal glass before retreating toward the couch. Gulping greedily, she pulled the glass away and looked at it appreciatively.

"Oh, God damn, that's good."

A tiny stream of sunlight beamed off the faceted surface perfectly, and a small dance of color and fire on the steel gray of the living room wall. First staring at the display in confusion, Raven quickly turned from it and looked around blankly at what had been her home with Donovan.

The sterile environment held no hint of her own personality. There were no colorful family photos on the walls, just black and white stills of her performances and glossy articles of him and his celebrity triumphs. In fact, the only actual photo in the living room was a twenty by twenty-eight close-up of their wedding day. She staggered a little and weaved over to it, not noticing the red wine sluicing over the rim of the glass and onto the floor. A candid one taken in a stolen moment when white rose petals fluttered all around them. He was turned toward the crowd, handsome and confident, laughing and waving but she had looked at the camera, caught in an expression of— what? Revelation? Fear? Uncertainty? She looked at it, blearily trying to identify the emotion. Did some part of her already know it was destined to damnation? She was quite sure he'd chosen the photo because of how he looked in it, which was terrific, and probably hadn't even noticed her expression. How come she, herself, was only really seeing it for the first time now?

Upon their first meeting, Raven, hired to give one of her first performances, played her original music at an art show. The floors and fixtures, glossy and expensive under the lights, featured beautiful glass creations, from a local but world-renowned glass-smith. The beauty in his talent reflected in her music.

Donovan, nearly twenty years her senior, stopped to listen appearing mesmerized.

"You play well," he remarked. "How long have you been performing?"

"Um, not very long. I guess, maybe, about a year," she admitted, embarrassed to say it was her first major gig.

Fortner seemed to read the story in her starry-eyed look immediately, and the corners of his mouth turned up. He reached into his pocket, withdrawing a small, slim titanium container, and pulled out a business card, extending it to her with an elegant, manicured hand.

"My name is Donovan Fortner. I am the owner of Fortner Talent and Publicity, downtown." He nodded at her to accept the card. "I want you to call there tomorrow and set up a meeting with my assistant Monica, to discuss some possible options for you."

"Oh," Raven replied, a little breathless. "Um, sure... thank you."

He merely nodded and returned his attention to the stunning young brunette he'd brought as his date. Raven stared after him. He was tall, trim, and resplendent in a charcoal suit, with a blood-red tie, in a perfect Windsor knot. His hair had streaks of silver at the temples, and his dark gray eyes were cool, appraising, and intelligent.

She made an appointment, and he'd signed her to his agency that very day. Tremendously talented in his chosen profession, and highly respected in the industry,

Donovan never let her forget who would be in charge, beginning from their initial meeting.

She would stare into the mirror as her golden tresses were saturated the raven color of her name, freckles covered in heavy makeup, and her lush body packaged for show business. He mocked and questioned her tastes and choices. As the performances grew and her name became known, she transformed into the superstar he alone envisioned. Stage presence, costumes and set designs, backup singers, dancers, and of course, the music, all became decisions made exclusively by the older man.

"Raven, I need to talk to you about your sets. The touchy-feely, unplugged music isn't your niche. It's not your brand."

"Brand?"

"Yes," he said, sighing at her ignorance. "A brand. What people associate with you. Your genre of music must captivate the younger audience. That means your look, music, act, attitude, press—everything gears toward selling to that market. Honestly, Raven, we've gone over this several times."

In fact, they hadn't, but she didn't want another argument she wouldn't win. "Well, why can't I just write something to fit that brand?"

"Because I don't think your talent extends that far." Donovan hadn't attempted to hide his condescension. "I think we have far more talented and highly motivated writers. You will be playing their offerings."

"But—"

"Do not argue with me," he snapped, exasperated. "Christ, I've been doing this a very long time. You have not and need to trust my expertise. Do you understand me?"

Raven had simply nodded. He was probably right. What she liked to listen to and create wasn't necessarily what others wanted to hear. Trusting him to understand far better what was right for her success in the industry, she always acquiesced. He began taking her on lunch dates, quiet dinners, lavish theater productions, and finally, bed. They were married two years later when she turned twenty-one.

Now, thirteen years later, she was amazed that two fat tears could still leak from her eyes, and once more started for the couch. The light hit the facets of her glass again, and the color exploded even more forcefully from the crystal. She stared in fascination that the sun could create that kind of light, color, and power. She didn't have power, color, or light anymore, if she ever had it in the first place. Thinking for a moment and looking at the glass, she decided there was color in her music. From nowhere she turned and violently hurled the glass onto the wedding photo, shattering the crystal and splattering the clean surfaces with claret. She screamed out her frustration and anger until she lay down on the couch and the afternoon turned to night.

"*Oh,* my Lord," Que sang as she opened Raven's door with her key, then threw it onto the small entry table. Hesitantly, she walked into the living room, glass crunching underneath her feet. Scanning for the source, she noticed the ruined photo and furniture. Drawing back, she nodded, as if to say, *yeah okay, I'm fine with that.* Que walked back to her friend's bedroom, to find Raven lying on the floor.

"Oh *hell* no." She walked over to Raven and brushed her greasy black hair from her face. "What in the hell you doin', girl?" Raven groaned but didn't open her eyes, pissing her friend off even more. "Raven!"

"What?" she croaked.

"What is this? Come on now." Que helped her stand up, saying, "Get your skinny white ass up off this floor." Becoming vertical turned Raven puce. Que jerked back quickly, stating with emphatic attitude, "I know you ain't gonna hurl on me." Then peered at her patient dubiously.

"Ugh..." The room spun wildly, and Raven's mouth turned down in anticipation of throwing up.

Que half-dragged the troubled woman onto her bed, then moved quickly to the bathroom for a cold cloth, water, and some pain reliever. She knelt in front of her and began to wash her face. Raven took in her best friend's natural corkscrew afro, in a stylish puff around her beautiful cocoa-colored face. Big red pouty lips and the kindest, deepest mahogany eyes she'd ever seen, tried to smile back at her.

"I know you're hurtin', honey." Que took a deep breath and clucked, as she wiped away some of the tears streaking Raven's face. "Papers are signed, all official, what're you gonna do now, it's all scary..." She considered Raven's incredibly large, troubled, baby-blue eyes, framed by long, dark, wet lashes. "But there's a reason this happened, baby. There's a reason this man wasn't for you. God has a plan, and we aren't smart enough to know it."

"But what am I supposed to do now, Que?" Raven looked miserably at her friend. "He manages me. He runs it all. He's in charge of everything. I don't know how to do the stuff." She looked out the window. "I know, I should. The whole thing was just so stupid. I should've paid attention. It was just so easy to let him do it. I'm just so...stupid."

"You aren't stupid. A little naïve maybe, but baby you're supposed to be able to trust your husband. Here." Que shook two tablets into her hand and gave Raven the glass of water. "I want you to take these and drink this."

Raven pushed back her hair absently, swallowed the medication, then closed her eyes, waiting for relief.

"You know Rave, you guys have been goin' through this process for a while now. Why're you still doin' this to yourself?" When she didn't answer, Que stood up and walked toward the kitchen. "I'm gonna make you something to eat."

"I'm not hungry."

"Tough shit, you'll eat it. Now go take a shower, cause girl, you stink. And get dressed."

Raven followed her best friend with her gaze, groaned, then walked into the bathroom. Closing the door, she stripped down and tried to focus on her image reflected in the mirror. Mascara from the day before streaked down her tired face, and she had lost weight in the last eight months. Closing her eyes, she mentally berated herself. She didn't love the man anymore, so why was this so hard? Why did she let him have such control over her? Moaning, she stepped into the shower and let the scalding hot water rain down over her. The cold, wet tile of the shower beckoned, and she pressed her forehead to it, remembering what started her on this course.

That night, Amanda, one of Raven's previous backup singers, also managed by Donovan, held a reception to launch her own independent career. Raven, in search of a restroom, mistakenly opened the wrong door, to a darkened room. There she witnessed her husband kissing Amanda, one hand on the woman's face and another under her shirt and on her breast. Both looked up when the sliver of light from the doorway widened. Donovan's brows rose, more impatient than chastened.

"Yes, Raven, may I help you?" When she just stood there with her mouth open, he offered casually, "Oh, of course. Raven, I think you remember Amanda." She looked at the woman.

"Hey Raven," Amanda said, having the decency to look sheepish.

"Ah." Raven let out the breath, she'd been holding. "Good evening, Amanda," she said stupidly, then looked blankly at her husband.

"Yes, well," Donovan said, taking his conquest's hand and approaching his wife. "This is significantly awkward, and we'll discuss it later tonight."

He walked back out into the party without letting go of Amanda's hand, making Raven's humiliation complete. And that had been it. Donovan came home, smelling of the young starlet's perfume, saying he'd given the matter some thought and felt his marriage had run its course. When Raven asked him if he had ever loved her, he laughed.

"Raven, I told you, it's ridiculous. A bored housewife's illusion created by greeting cards and bleeding hearts." He rolled his eyes and chuckled, then noticed her stricken face. "Yes, okay, if you need to hear that to cope with this challenge. Yes, darling, I loved you. I believe we have benefitted each other tremendously and I will, of course, continue to manage you, if you wish. In fact, you'll need my help, at least to transition."

Then he exited the condo and didn't return, leaving her to wonder when he had turned so cruel. Why hadn't she seen that condescension before, that absolute control and equally absolute indifference? It was as if she were no more than a pesky fly he had finally swatted.

After her shower, Raven brushed her teeth and hair, then stood in front of her closet, trying to decide what one wears when they start their life over. She dragged on her most frayed, hole-ridden pair of blue jeans and a threadbare navy-blue hoody, just because she knew he'd hate it. After lacing up a pair of beaten-up tennis shoes, she walked back to her kitchen. Que had cleaned up the wine and lain fruit and some cheese on a plate at the kitchen island. The bag she brought it in was neatly folded on the counter.

"Here, start with this. I'm gonna make some lunch, and then we're all gonna have a talk." "All?"

"Yeah," Que said, "you, me, and him."

She nodded toward the dining room table, where Raven's twin brother, Wyatt, sat pretending to read the paper. Raven was elated. He stood up and opened his arms to envelop her. Laying her head on his chest, she listened to his steady heartbeat, as he kissed the top of her head.

"What the fuck're you doin'?" he murmured.

"I'm trying to learn how to be a divorced woman whose husband cheated on her in front of the whole damn world."

"How 'bout you become a divorced woman that doesn't give a shit." He tried to look her in the face, but she hugged him harder. "Preferably one that learns how to stand on her own two feet?"

"Because one involves wallowing and one involves hard, painful work."

"You've done that before. I think you're up to it." Wyatt tilted her head up to his and kissed her forehead. "Don't ya think?"

"Lunch is served," Que sang, setting a plate with an enormous sandwich on the counter. She reached for two smaller ones and gestured for the twins to sit. "So," Que said, sitting down herself, "where to go, what to do from here?"

"What d'ya wanna do, Rave?" Wyatt asked, taking a large bite of his lunch.

"I don't know, go on vacation?" she teased. Both her guests looked at one another and grinned in epiphany. She eyed them both. "What?"

"A vacation?" Wyatt asked.

"Oh yes," Que said.

"Vacation? No, I was kidding. Didn't you hear what I said before, Que? I have to figure all this out. He's overseen everything, and the one thing I do know is that I don't want him to be my manager anymore, which means I don't have one. Which means I'm going to have to find one that isn't nasty, greedy, or incompetent. I don't know what gigs he's been promised. He was supposed to…"

"What better way to figure it all out?" Wyatt placated. "Go someplace warm and lay on a beach."

"Or better yet, just get laid," Que suggested, as Wyatt winced.

"Laid!" Raven laughed. "I just got divorced."

"Yeah, but it's been happening over eight months, and I'm bettin' it was a significant amount of time before that since you've been getting' any. Something tells me Cap'n Sugar Britches wasn't that good at it anyway. It'll relax you."

Raven laughed at Que's nickname for Donovan. Where her ex-husband had tolerated Wyatt, he vehemently hated her best friend. The feeling was extremely mutual.

"Um, can we stop talking about this?" Wyatt suggested, looking between the two. "Seriously, I don't want to hear about it." Both women continued to giggle but agreed to let it go.

"I do know it's been damn near a decade since you've had a decent vacation," Que stated.

"That's not true. I've been everywhere."

"To perform, maybe, but not to just hang out," Wyatt interjected.

"Where's the one place you've never been?" her friend asked, trying to keep her on track. "Someplace you've always wanted to go to?" Enjoying herself, Raven turned pink.

"You'll think it's stupid."

"No, I won't," both said in unison.

"I've never been to Hawai'i."

"Hawai'i?" Que's brow furrowed. "That's here. Don't you wanna go to, like, the Bahamas or something? How have you not been to Hawai'i?"

"Donovan always wanted to play the massive arenas and big cities, and for some unfathomable reason that didn't include the islands."

"You should do it then. Take some time, figure some shit out."

"What about my tour dates?"

"You'll get 'em from dickhead or whoever, then call and cancel them. Hell, you can even interview new people to run the works while you're there. You're in the position to do that now, Rave. People would fall all over themselves to come to you. The point is to go away and figure it all out."

She bit her bottom lip and thought about all the problems this idea would bring until her brother spoke the next words.

"What're you afraid of Rave? What do you have to lose?"

Purchase Jeny's Books:
https://bit.ly/3uxIDcA